A PERMANENT
MEMBER
OF THE
FAMILY

Also by Russell Banks

A PERMANENT MEMBER OF THE FAMILY

RUSSELL BANKS

Alfred A. Knopf Canada

PUBLISHED BY KNOPF CANADA

Copyright © 2013 Russell Banks

www.randomhouse.ca

Library and Archives Canada Cataloguing in Publication

Banks, Russell, 1940–
    A permanent member of the family : selected stories / Russell Banks.

Short stories.
Also issued in electronic format.

ISBN 978-0-345-80812-7

    I. Title.

PS3552.A46P47 2013   813'.54   C2013-901638-4

Designed by Suet Yee Chong
Jacket design by Allison Saltzman
Jacket photograph © by Colleen Farrell/Arcangel Images

Printed and bound in the United States of America

10 9 8 7 6 5 4 3 2 1

To Chase

and

in memory, Kili (2000–2013)

CONTENTS

ACKNOWLEDGMENTS

Some of these stories were first published in the following periodicals: *Conjunctions* ("A Permanent Member of the Family"); *Esquire* ("The Outer Banks"); *Harper's* ("Christmas Party"); *Libération* ("Lost and Found," translated by Pierre Furlan); *Narrative* ("Lost and Found"); *Salmagundi* ("Big Dog"); *Yale Review* ("Blue," "Transplant").

"The Invisible Parrot" was first published in *Fighting Words* (Dublin, 2012), a limited-edition anthology edited by Roddy Doyle.

FORMER MARINE

After lying in bed awake for an hour, Connie finally pushes
back the blankets and gets up. It's still dark. He's barefoot and
shivering in his boxers and T-shirt and a little hungover from
one beer too many at 20 Main last night. He snaps the bedside
lamp on and resets the thermostat from fifty-five to sixty-five.
The burner makes a huffing sound and the fan kicks in, and
the smell of kerosene drifts through the trailer. He pats his new
hearing aids into place and peers out the bedroom window.
Snow is falling across a pale splash of lamplight on the lawn. It's
a week into April and it ought to be rain, but Connie is glad it's
snow. He removes his .45-caliber Colt service pistol from the
drawer of the bedside table, checks to be sure it's loaded and
lays it on the dresser.

By the time he has shaved and dressed and driven to town

in his pickup, three and a half inches of heavy wet snow have accumulated. The town plows and salt trucks are already out. The plate glass windows of the M & M Diner are fogged over, and from the street you can't see the half-dozen men and two women inside eating breakfast and making low-voiced, sporadic conversation with one another.

By choice, Connie sits alone at the back of the room, reading the sports section of the Plattsburgh *Press-Republican*. He has known everyone in the place personally for most of their lives. They are all on their way to work. He, however, is not. He calls himself the Retiree, even though he never officially retired from anything and nobody else calls him the Retiree. Eight months ago he was let go by Ray Piaggi at Ray's Auction House. Let go. Like he was a helium-filled balloon on a string, he tells people. He sometimes adds that you know the economy is in trouble when even auctioneers start cutting back, indicating that it's not his fault he's unemployed, using food stamps, on Medicaid, scraping by on social security and unemployment benefits that are about to run out. It's the economy's fault. And the fault of whoever the hell's in charge of it.

Connie has already ordered his usual breakfast—scrambled eggs, sausage patty, toasted English muffin and coffee—when his eldest son, Jack, comes through the door. Jack nods and smiles hello to the other diners like a man running for office and pats the waitress, Vivian, on the shoulder. He shucks his heavy gray bomber jacket and pulls off his winter trooper hat, hangs them on a wall hook next to his dad's Carhartt and forest green fleece balaclava, and takes the seat facing the door, opposite his dad.

"I was starting to think it was time to pack that stuff away," Jack says.

Connie says, "One of my goddam hearing aids just told me, 'Battery low.' Like I can't tell when it's dead and that's why I'm getting no reception. Man my age, his batteries are always low, for chrissake. I don't need no hearing aid to tell me."

"Your hearing aids talk to you?"

"It's a way to get me to buy new batteries before I really need them. I'll probably buy fifty extra batteries a year, one a week, just to get my goddam hearing aids to stop telling me my battery's low."

"Seriously, Dad, your hearing aids talk to you? You hearing voices?"

"Yeah, I'm a regular schizo. No, it's these new computerized units Medicaid won't subsidize. Over six grand! I shouldn't have listened to that goddam audiologist and bought the subsidized cheapos instead. With these, there's a little lady inside whispers that your battery's low. Also tells you what channel you're on. I got five channels with these units—for listening to music, for quiet time, reverse focus and what they call master. Master's the human conversational channel. And there's also one for phone. I can't tell the difference between any of 'em, except phone, which when you're not actually talking on the phone is like a goddam echo chamber. It does help me hear with a cell phone, though."

Vivian sets Connie's platter of food and coffee in front of him. "That gonna be it, Conrad?"

"Please, Viv, for chrissake, don't call me Conrad. Only my ex-wife called me Conrad, and thankfully I haven't heard it from her in nearly thirty years."

"I'm kidding," she says without looking at him. "Connie," she adds. She takes Jack's order, oatmeal with milk and a cup of coffee, and heads back to the kitchen. For a few seconds, while his father digs into his breakfast, Jack studies the man. Jack's been a state trooper for twelve years and studies people's behavior, even his seventy-year-old father's, with a learned, calm detachment. "You seem sort of agitated this morning, Dad. Everything okay?"

"Yeah, sure. I was just teasing Viv about that Conrad business. But it is true, y'know, only your mother called me that. She used it to give me orders or criticize me. Like she was afraid I'd take advantage of her somehow if she got friendly enough to call me Connie."

"You probably would've."

"Yeah, well, your mother took off before I really had a chance to take advantage of her. Smart gal. She quit before I could fire her."

"That's one way to look at it."

"You have to let it go, Jack. She didn't want the job, and I did. In the end, everybody, including you boys, got what they needed."

"You're right, Dad. You're right." They've had this exchange a hundred times.

Vivian sets Jack's coffee and oatmeal in front of him and scoots away as if a little scared of Connie, mocking him. Jack smiles agreeably after her and shakes out the front section of the newspaper and scans the headlines while he eats. Connie goes back to the sports page.

Jack says, "Looks like we got through March without another bank robbery. Maybe our boy has headed south, like Butch Cassidy and the Sundance Kid." He flips the front page over and goes on to national news.

After a few minutes, without looking up, Connie says, "You talk to Buzz and Chip recently?"

Jack looks over at his father as if expecting more, then says, "No, not in the last few days."

"Everything the same with them these days?"

"More or less. Far as I know."

"Wives and kids?"

"Yep, the same, far as I know. All is well. No news is good news, Dad."

"I wouldn't mind any kind of news, actually."

"They're busy, Dad. It's easier for me, I don't have a wife and kids. Plus Buzz has that long drive every day up to Dannemora and back, and Chip's taking criminal justice courses nights at North Country Community College down in Ticonderoga. And they both live way the hell over in Keeseville. Don't take it personally, Dad."

"I don't," Connie says and goes back to reading the sports page.

Jack finishes his oatmeal, shoves his bowl to one side and cups his mug of coffee in his large red hands, warming them. He's thinking. He suddenly asks, "You ever consider it a little weird that all three of us went into law enforcement? I sometimes wonder about it. I mean, it isn't like you were a police officer. Like me and Chip. Or a prison guard like Buzz. I mean, you ran auctions."

"Yeah, but don't forget, I'm a former Marine. And you're never an ex-Marine, Jack. So that was the standard you boys were raised by, the United States Marine Corps standard, especially after your mother took off. If my father had been a former Marine, I probably would have gone into law enforcement too. I always kind of regretted none of you boys were Marines."

"Dad, you can't regret something someone else did or didn't do. Only what you yourself did or didn't do."

Connie smiles and says, "See, that's exactly the sort of thing a former Marine would say!"

Jack smiles back. The old man amuses him. But he worries him too. The old man's in denial about his finances, Jack thinks. He's got to be worse than broke. Jack gets up from the table, walks to the counter and tries to pay Vivian for both their breakfasts, but Connie sees what he's up to. He jumps from his seat and slides between his son and the waitress, waving a twenty-dollar bill in her face, insisting on paying for both his and Jack's meals.

Vivian shrugs and takes Connie's twenty, just to get it out of her face.

She hands him his change, and father and son walk back to the table, where both men pull their coats and hats on. "You take care of the tip," Connie says. "Make it big enough so you and I come out even and Vivian ends up forgiving me for being an asshole."

"Dad, you sure you're okay? I mean, financially? It's got to be a little rough these days."

Connie doesn't answer, except to make a pulled-down face designed to tell his son he sounds ridiculous. Absurd. Of course he's okay financially. He's the father. Still the man of the house. A former Marine.

IT'S A THIRTY-MILE DRIVE from Au Sable Forks to Lake Placid, forty-five minutes in good weather, twice that today. The roads are plowed and passable but slick all the way over—slowing to a creep through Wilmington Notch, where the altitude is more than two thousand feet and the falling snow is nearing whiteout.

It's a quarter to ten when Connie pulls his white, two-

wheel-drive Ford Ranger into Cold Brook Plaza. He's filled the
bed of the truck with a quarter ton of bagged gravel to give the
vehicle traction in weather like this. The truck is seven years
old with a rust belt under the doors and along the seams of the
bed. He parks it off to the windowless side of the Lake Placid
branch of the Adirondack Bank, a low pop-up building not
much larger than a double-wide. There are no other vehicles
in the parking area. Nobody's using the drive-through or the
ATM. He notices in the employees' lot behind the building a
new Subaru Outback and one of those humpbacked Pontiac
SUVs he hates looking at because they're so ugly.

The windshield wipers bump across runnels of ice forming on the glass, and he knows he should get out there with a
scraper and clear the ice, but decides to let the defroster heat
the glass from inside and melt it. He can't linger. Too easy to
run into someone he knows, even this far from home. He sets
the emergency brake, grabs the green gym bag off the floor beside him and steps from the truck, leaving the motor running
and the defroster and heater on high. He walks around the
truck, making sure that both license plates are covered in hard-
ened road-slush. When he gets to the bank entrance, he turns
away for a second and yanks down his fleece balaclava, trans-
forming it into a ski mask, a not unusual sight on a snowy day in
a ski town like Lake Placid. Then he pulls open the heavy glass
door and enters the bank.

There are two slender young tellers behind the chest-high

counter, girls in their early twenties who appear to be counting money back there, and a middle-aged bank officer standing at the open door of her glassed-in cubicle. All three offer him a welcoming gaze when he comes through the door—the first customer of the day. The bank officer holds a notary stamp press in her hands as if it's a precious gift. She's a redheaded, round-faced woman wearing a two-piece green wool suit and tangerine-colored blouse. To Connie she looks like a social worker, the kind who interviewed him for Medicaid and food stamps. That humpbacked Pontiac is probably hers. The tellers are dressed more casually, in matching gray pleated skirts, black tights, long-sleeved button-down shirts and fleece vests. They both have mud-colored shoulder-length hair and rosy cheeks. Connie thinks they must be twins and dress alike on purpose. Buzz and Chip, who are twins, used to do that in high school. Just to confuse people, he remembers. These girls are a little old for that.

He leans back against the counter and says to the bank officer, "Would you look at this, please?" He puts his left hand deep into his jacket pocket and holds out the gym bag with his right. She comes up to him, and he hands her the open bag.

She furrows her brow, puzzled, wary, but places the notary stamp press on the counter anyhow, takes the bag and peers into it. It's empty, except for five words hand-printed in capital letters with a black Magic Marker on a white sheet of paper: FILL WITH CASH. OWNER ARMED.

"Oh, dear," she says. She takes the gym bag and, avoiding his eyes, passes through the low gate and goes behind the counter where the confused tellers stand and watch.

Connie says to the tellers, "You girls just step back a few feet from the counter there and don't touch anything. Keep your hands where I can see them. This'll all be over in a minute." To the white-faced bank officer he says, "Less than a minute, actually. Thirty seconds. I'm counting," he says and commences to count backward from thirty. By the time he reaches twelve, she has emptied the contents of the cash drawers into the gym bag. She zips the bag closed and passes it to him.

It's nice and heavy, about three pounds of money, he guesses. He thanks her with a nod and, still counting out loud, backs quickly away from the counter toward the door, right hand holding the gym bag, left hand deep in his jacket pocket clasping the grip of his reliable old Colt M1911 service pistol. At five he is outside the bank, and at one he's in his truck, then releasing the hand brake, and he has backed the truck up and turned, unseen, and headed west out of town on Old Military Road.

In the falling snow traffic is light and slow moving. A mile beyond the city limits, where the road enters the hamlet of Ray Brook, a pair of state police cruisers, their lights flashing, speeds toward him, and he pulls slightly off to the right to let them zoom past. A minute later he passes the Ray Brook state police headquarters, where until a year ago his son Jack was stationed. If Jack were headquartered there today, he'd likely be driving one of those cruisers that just blew by, and he might have recognized his dad's white, rusted-out Ford Ranger and wondered what he was doing way over here. But Jack's stationed in Au Sable Forks now, not Ray Brook, and that's why, after robbing four branches of three different banks in Essex and Franklin Counties in the last seven months, Connie has waited until now to rob the Lake Placid branch of the Adirondack Bank and why afterward he drove west, away from Au Sable Forks and home. He doesn't want his sons to ask him any questions that he can't answer truthfully.

He drives through the town of Saranac Lake, looping via Route 3 gradually north toward Plattsburgh, where he spends the rest of the morning into the afternoon hanging out at the Champlain Centre mall like a bored teenager. With the gym bag locked in the pickup in the parking lot and the money uncounted, unexamined—for all he knows it could be three pounds of one-dollar bills, although more likely it's tens, twenties, fifties and hundreds, like the others—he roams through the tool department at Sears and drifts on to the food court, where he eats Chinese food, and then goes to a 2:00 P.M. screening of *Lincoln,* which he likes in spite of being surprised that Abraham Lincoln had such a high, squeaky voice. While he's watching the movie, the temperature outside rises into the mid-thirties and the falling snow dwindles and finally stops. It's almost 5:00 P.M. when he comes blinking out of the multiplex and decides it's safe now to drive back to Au Sable Forks.

The six-lane Northway is puddled with salted snowmelt and slush. In Keeseville, still ten miles from home, he exits from the turnpike on the wide, sweeping off-ramp to Route 9N. Keeseville is where his two younger sons and their families live and is not so damned far from Au Sable Forks that they couldn't drop by to visit once a month if they wanted to, he thinks, and in order to power the truck through the curve, Connie guns it. The quarter ton of bagged gravel in the truck bed has shifted the weight of the vehicle from the front tires to the rear, and the centrifugal pull of the turn causes the rear tires to lose their grip on the pavement and slip sideways to the left. Connie automatically flips the steering wheel to the left, the direction of the slide, but the rear end whipsaws back to the right, putting the truck into a slow 180-degree spin, back to front, until he's facing the way he's come and the truck is sliding sideways and downhill toward the off-ramp guardrail at about forty miles an hour.

It's only a concussion and a busted collarbone, Jack explains to his father. But the collarbone broke in two places and as a result is in three separate pieces. "They called in one of the sports docs from Lake Placid, guy who works on ski accidents all the time. He operated and put pins in it, but given your age and bone loss, he doesn't think the pins'll hold if you get hit in that area again. He said you'll have to protect your right side like it's made of glass."

"How long was I out?" Connie asks. He's just realized that Chip and Buzz are in the room, standing somewhere behind Jack. He's woozy and confused about where he is exactly, although he can tell it's a hospital room. He's in a bed with an IV stuck in his arm and an empty bed next to his and a chair in the corner and a window with the curtain pulled back. It's dark outside.

"You were out when I got to the truck, which was no more than ten minutes after the accident, I'd guess. A citizen with a cell phone in a car right behind you saw the truck go over and called 911. I happened to be driving north on 87 just below the exit. You came to in the ambulance, but they knocked you out when you went in for surgery. You don't remember the ambulance and all that?"

"Last thing I remember is the truck going into a slide. Hello, boys," he says to Chip and Buzz. "Sorry to bring you out like this." They look worried, brows furrowed, unsmiling, both in uniform, Buzz in his Dannemora prison guard's uniform and Chip in his Plattsburgh police officer blues. All three of his sons wear uniforms well. He likes that. "Hope you didn't have to leave work for this."

Chip says that he was on duty, but since that had him here in Plattsburgh, it was no big deal to come right over to the hospital, and Buzz says that he was just getting home when Jack called, so it was no big deal for him, either, to drive back to Plattsburgh. "Edie sends her love," Buzz adds.

"Yeah, Joan sends love, too, Dad," Chip says.

Connie asks about his truck. He has just remembered the gym bag.

Jack says, "Totaled. Northway Sunoco came over and towed it out. You really put it all the way off the ramp and into the woods. Thicket of small birches stopped you. Good thing it wasn't a full-grown tree or you'd have gone through the windshield. You weren't wearing a seat belt. Where were you coming from?"

"Plattsburgh. The movies at Champlain mall. I wanted to see that movie about Abraham Lincoln everybody's talking about."

All four men are silent for a moment, as if each is lost in his own thoughts. Finally Chip says, "Dad, we've got to ask you a couple of tough questions." Jack and Buzz nod in agreement.

Connie's heart is racing. He knows what's coming.

Chip says, "It's about the money in the bag."

"What bag?"

Jack says, "The EMT guys gave me the bag, Dad, the gym bag, when they pulled you out of the truck. I didn't open it till after you were in surgery. I wasn't prying. I opened it in case there was a bottle in it that might've broke or something. Although I don't think you were drinking," he adds.

"No, I wasn't! Not a drop all day! It was the snow and ice on the road that did it."

Chip says, "We need to know where you got the money, Dad. There's a lot of it. Thousands of dollars."

Buzz says, "And we need to know why you were carrying your forty-five."

"It's not illegal," Connie says to him. "Not yet, anyhow."

Jack says, "But the gun and the money, they're connected, aren't they, Dad? I've been putting two and two together, you know. Connecting the dots, like they say. For instance, wondering where you got the money for those hearing aids that Medicaid wouldn't pay for."

"I'm doing okay money-wise. I had some savings, you know."

Buzz says, "I know what goes on inside prison, Dad. It's worse than anything you can imagine. I don't want you there. But you're looking at hard time. Armed robbery. You'll be there the rest of your goddam life. What the Christ were you thinking?"

Of the three Buzz is the only one who looks sad. Jack's face and Chip's show no emotion, not even curiosity, but that's because they're trained police officers. Connie says, "I don't know what you guys are talking about."

Buzz says, "Dad, what the hell do you want us to do? What

do you think we should do? What's the right thing here, Dad?"

"You don't have to do anything. As an American citizen I can carry my service pistol if I want, and I can carry my money around in cash in a goddam gym bag if I want. Who can trust the goddam banks these days anyhow?"

Jack says, "It's not your money! It belongs to the Adirondack Bank branch in Lake Placid that was robbed this morning. Robbed by a guy in a ski mask and a Carhartt jacket with a gym bag that had a note in it that said, 'Fill with cash, owner armed.' The note's still in the bottom of the bag, Dad. Under the money. I checked."

"You checked? So you were snooping? Invading my privacy?"

Buzz says, "Jesus Christ, Dad, make sense! There's two of us standing here who can arrest you! Is that what you want? To be arrested by your own sons? And make the third your prison guard?"

Connie looks across the room at the window and through the glass into the darkness beyond. He wonders if it's late at night or very early in the morning. He says, "Sounds funny when you put it that way. Like I wanted it to happen."

But it's not what he wanted to happen. When his sons were little boys and their mother abandoned them all so she could go off to live with an artist in a hippie commune in New Mexico, Connie held it together with discipline and devotion to duty. All by himself, he held the fort and took perfect fatherly care of his sons. And after they graduated high school he paid for Jack to go to college at Paul Smith's and for Buzz at Plattsburgh State for those two years when he wanted to be a radiologist. He paid for Chip's Hawaiian honeymoon with Joan. He even took care of them when they were in their early thirties by taking out a second mortgage and home equity loan, borrowing against his trailer and the land in Elizabethtown he inherited from his father, so his sons could buy their first houses. He wanted to take impeccable care of his sons, and he did. And after the boys grew up and no longer needed him to take care of them, he planned on continuing to hold the family together by being able to take impeccable care of himself. That was the long-range plan. They would still be a family, the four of them, and he would still be the father, the head of the household, because you're never an ex-father, any more than you're an ex-Marine.

But the way things turned out, he can't take care of himself. How can he explain this to his sons without them thinking he's pathetic and weak and stupid? First the real estate market tanked, and neither the trailer nor the land his father left him was worth as much as he owed on them, so even if he wanted to, he couldn't sell the properties for enough to pay off the loans and move into a government-subsidized room or studio apartment in town. Who'd buy his trailer and land anyhow? He'd still owe the banks tens of thousands of dollars and would have to go on making the monthly payments. Then he lost his job at

Ray's Auction House. Without it he could no longer make the payments to the banks, and when he missed two consecutive months, the banks' lawyers threatened to seize his trailer and the land. He was about to become an ex-father.

"How late is it?" he asks.

Jack says, "Late. Quarter of three."

"What do you want us to do, Dad?" Buzz says again.

Connie asks them what they've done with the money, and Jack says it's still in the gym bag, which he put on the shelf in the closet of the hospital room, where they hung his clothes and coat.

"What about my service pistol? Where's it at?" A man's gun is not to be disturbed, especially when the man is your father and a former Marine.

"It's in the bag with the money," Buzz says.

"So nobody else knows about this yet, except for you three?"

Jack says, "That's right."

Connie says, "Then nobody has to do anything about this tonight, right? It's late. You boys go get some sleep, and tomorrow the three of you sit down together and decide what you want to do. It's your decision, not mine. I know that whatever you do, boys, it'll be the right thing. It's what I raised you to do."

They seem relieved and exhale almost in unison, as if all three have been holding their breath. Buzz reaches down and tousles the old man's thin, sandy gray hair, as if ruffling the fur of a favorite dog. He says, "Okay. Sounds like a plan, Dad."

"Yeah," Chip says. "Sounds like a plan."

Jack nods agreement. He's the first out the door, and the others quickly follow. They catch up to him in the hallway, and the three walk side by side in silence to the elevator. They remain silent in the elevator and down two floors and all the way out to the parking lot. They stop beside Jack's cruiser for a second and look back and up at the large square window of their father's room. A nurse draws the blind closed, and the light in the room goes out.

Jack opens the door on the driver's side and gets in. "You want to meet for breakfast and figure out what's next?"

"Where?" Chip asks. "I've got the noon-to-nine shift, so breakfast is good."

"M & M in Au Sable Forks at eight? The old man's favorite breakfast joint."

"I can make it okay," Buzz says, "but I have to be on the road to Dannemora by nine."

Chip says, "I guess we already know what's next, don't we?"

Buzz says, "His pistol, is it loaded?"

"I didn't check," Jack says, getting out of the car. Buzz is already walking very fast back toward the hospital entrance, and Chip is running to catch up, when from their father's room on the second floor they hear the gunshot.

A PERMANENT MEMBER
OF THE FAMILY

I'm not sure I want to tell this story on myself, not now, some thirty-five years after it happened. But it has more or less become a family legend and consequently has been much revised and, if I may say, since I'm not merely a witness to the crime but its presumed perpetrator, much distorted as well. It has been told around by people who are virtual strangers, people who heard it from one of my daughters, or my son-in-law or my granddaughter, all of whom enjoy telling it because it paints the old man, that's me, in a somewhat humiliating light. Apparently, humbling the old man still gives pleasure, and not just to people who know him personally.

My main impulse here is merely to set the record straight, even if it does in a vague way reflect badly on me. Not on my character so much as on my ability to anticipate bad things and thus on my ability to have protected my children when they were very young from those bad things. I'm also trying to reclaim the story, to take it back and make it mine again. If that sounds selfish of me, remember that for thirty-five years it has belonged to everyone else.

It was the winter following the summer I separated from Louise, the woman who for fourteen turbulent years had been my wife. It took place in a shabbily quaint village in southern New Hampshire where I was teaching literature at a small liberal arts college. The divorce had not yet kicked in, but the separation was complete, an irreversible fact of life—my life and Louise's and the lives of our three girls, Andrea, Caitlin and Sasha, who were six, nine and thirteen years old. My oldest daughter, Vickie, from my first marriage, was then eighteen and living with me, having run away from her mother and stepfather's home in North Carolina. She was enrolled as a freshman at the college where I taught and was temporarily housed in a studio apartment I built for her above the garage. All of us were fissioned atoms spun off nuclear families, seeking new, recombinant nuclei.

I had left Louise in August and bought a small abandoned house with an attached garage, a quarter of a mile away, which felt and looked like the gatehouse to Louise's much larger, elaborately groomed Victorian manse on the hill. Following my departure, her social life, always more intense and open-ended than mine, continued unabated and even intensified, as if for years my presence had acted as a party killer. On weekends especially, cars rumbled back and forth along the unpaved lane between my cottage and her house at all hours of the day and night. Some of the cars I recognized as belonging to our formerly shared friends; some of them were new to me and bore out-of-state plates.

We were each financially independent of the other, she through a sizable trust set up by her grandparents, I by virtue of my teaching position. There was, therefore, no alimony for our lawyers to fight for or against. Since our one jointly owned asset of consequence, that rather grandiose Victorian manse, had been purchased with her family's money, I signed my half of it over to her without argument. It had always seemed pretentiously bourgeois to me, a bit of an embarrassment, frankly, and I was glad to be rid of it.

Regarding the children, the plan was that my ex-wife, as I was already thinking of her, and I would practice "joint custody," a Solomonic solution to the rending of family fabric. At the time, the late 1970s, this was seen as a progressive, although mostly untried, way of doling out parental responsibilities in a divorce. Three and a half days a week the girls would reside with me and Vickie, and three and a half days a week with their mother. They would alternate three nights at my house one week with four nights the next, so that for every fourteen nights they would have slept seven at the home of each parent. Half their clothing and personal possessions would be at my place,

23

where I had carved two tiny, low-ceilinged bedrooms out of the attic, and half would be at their mother's, where each child had her own large, high-windowed bedroom and walk-in closet. It was an easy, safe stroll between the two houses, and on transitional days, the school bus could pick them up in the morning at one parent's house and drop them off that afternoon at the other. We agreed to handle the holidays and vacations on an ad hoc basis—postponing the problem, in other words.

That left only the cat, a large black Maine coon named Scooter, and the family dog, a white part-poodle mutt we'd rescued from the pound twelve years earlier when I was in graduate school. A neutered female unaccountably named Sarge, she was an adult dog of indeterminate age when we got her and was now very old. She was arthritic, half blind and partially deaf. And devoted to everyone in the family. We were her pack.

Louise and I agreed that Scooter and Sarge, unlike our daughters, could not adapt to joint custody and therefore would have to live full-time in one place or the other. I made a preemptive bid for Sarge, who was viewed as belonging not to either parent, but to the three girls, who were very protective of her, as if she were a mentally and physically challenged sibling. Despite her frailty, she was the perfect family dog: sweetly placid, utterly dependent and demonstrably grateful for any form of human kindness.

Scooter, on the other hand, was a loner and often out all night prowling the neighborhood for sex. We had neglected to castrate him until he was nearly three, and evidently he still thought he was obliged to endure mortal combat with other male cats for the sexual favors of females, even though he was no longer capable of enjoying those favors. He had long been regarded by Louise and the girls and by Scooter himself as my cat, probably because I was an early riser and fed him when he showed up at the back door at dawn looking like a boxer who needed a good cut man. And though neither of us overtly acknowledged it, he and I were the only males in the family. He ended up at my gatehouse down the lane not because I particularly wanted him there, but more or less by default.

In keeping with the principle of dividing custodial responsibilities equally between ex-husband and ex-wife, since the ex-husband had been claimed by the cat, it was decided that the dog would stay at the home of the ex-wife. She insisted on it. There was no discussion or negotiation. I balked at first, but then backed off. Keeping Sarge at her house was an important point of pride for Louise, the one small tilt in her favor in an otherwise equitable division of property, personal possessions and domestic responsibility. It was a small victory over me in a potentially much more destructive contest that we were both determined to avoid, and I didn't mind handing it to her. Choose your battles, I reminded myself. Also, claiming Sarge as her own was a not-so-subtle, though probably unconscious way for Louise to claim our daughters as more hers than mine. I didn't mind giving that to her, either, as long as I knew it was an illusion. It made me feel more magnanimous and wise than I really was.

Back then there were many differences between me and Louise as to reality and illusion, truth and falsity, and a frequent confusion of the causes of the breakdown of the marriage with the symptoms of an already broken marriage. But I'd rather not go into them here, because this story is not concerned with those differences and that confusion, which now these many years later have dwindled to irrelevance. Besides, both Louise and I have been happily remarried to new spouses for decades, and our children are practically middle-aged and have children of their own. One daughter is herself twice divorced. Like her dad.

At first the arrangement went as smoothly as Louise and I had hoped. The girls, bless their hearts, once the initial shock of the separation wore off, seemed to embrace the metronomic movement back and forth between their old familiar family home, now owned and operated solely by their mother, and the new, rough-hewn home operated by their father. With a swing set and slide from Sears, I turned the backyard into a suburban playground. It was a mild autumn with a long Indian summer, I recall, and I pitched a surplus army tent among the maples by the brook and let the girls grill hot dogs and toast marshmallows and sleep out there in sleeping bags on warm nights when there was no school the next day. Back in June, when I knew I'd soon be parenting and housekeeping on my own, I had scheduled my fall term classes and conferences for early in the day so that I could be home waiting for the girls when they stepped down from the bus. With Vickie living over the garage— although only sleeping there irregularly, as she now had a boy-friend at school who had his own apartment in town—my place that fall was like an after-school summer camp for girls.

The one unanticipated complication arose when Sarge trotted arthritically along behind the girls as best she could whenever they came from their mother's house to mine. This in itself was not a problem, except that, when the girls returned to their mother's at the end of their three or four scheduled nights with me, Sarge refused to follow. She stayed with me and Scooter. Her preference was clear, although her reasons were not. She even resisted being leashed and went limp like an antiwar demonstrator arrested for trespass and could not be made to stand and walk.

Within an hour of the girls' departure, Louise would telephone and insist that I drive the dog "home," as she put it. "Sarge lives with me," she said. "Me and the girls."

Custody of Sarge was a victory over Louise that I had not sought. I had never thought of her as "my" dog, but as the fam-ily dog, by which I meant belonging to the children. I tried ex-plaining that it appeared to be Sarge's decision to stay with me and assured her that I had done nothing to coerce the dog into staying and nothing to hinder her in any way from following the girls up the lane when they left. Quite the opposite.

But Louise would have none of it. "Just bring the damn

dog back. Now," she said and hung up. Her voice and her distinctive Virginia Tidewater accent echo in my ears these many years later.

I was driving a Ford station wagon then, and because of her arthritis poor old Sarge couldn't get into the back on her own, so I had to lift her up carefully and lay her in, and when I arrived at Louise's house, I had to open the tailgate and scoop the dog up in my arms and set her down on the driveway like an offering—a peace offering, I suppose, though it felt more like a propitiation.

This happened every week. Despite all Louise's efforts to keep Sarge a permanent resident of her house, the dog always managed to slip out, arriving at my door just behind the girls, or else she came down the lane, increasingly, on her own, even when the girls were in their mother's custody. So it wasn't Andrea, Caitlin and Sasha that the dog was following, it was me. I began to see that in her canine mind I was her pack leader, and since I had moved to a new den, so had she. If she didn't follow me there, she'd be without a leader and a proper den.

There was nothing that Louise and I could do to show Sarge how wrong she was. She wasn't wrong, of course; she was a dog. Finally, after about a month, Louise gave up, although she never announced her capitulation. Simply, there came a time when my ex-wife no longer called me with orders to deliver our family dog to her doorstep.

Everyone—me, Sarge, the girls, I think even Louise—was

relieved. We all knew on some level that a major battle, one with a likelihood of causing considerable collateral damage, had been narrowly avoided. Yet, despite my relief, I felt a buzzing, low-grade anxiety about having gained sole custody of Sarge. I wasn't aware of it then, but looking back now I see that Sarge, as long as she was neither exclusively mine nor Louise's, functioned in our newly disassembled family as the last remaining link to our preseparation, prelapsarian past, to a time of relative innocence, when all of us, but especially the girls, still believed in the permanence of our family unit, our pack.

If Sarge had only agreed to traipse up and down the lane behind the girls, if she had agreed to accept joint custody, then my having left my wife could have been seen by all of us as an eccentric, impulsive, possibly even temporary, sleeping arrangement, and for the girls it could have been a bit like going on a continuous series of neighborhood camping trips with Dad. I would not have felt quite so guilty, and Louise would not have been so hurt and angry. The whole abandonment issue would have been ameliorated somewhat. The children would not have been so traumatized; their lives, as they see them today, would not have been permanently disfigured, and neither Louise nor I might have gone looking so quickly for replacement spouses.

That's a lot of weight to put on a family dog, I know. We all lose our innocence soon enough; it's inescapable. Most of us aren't emotionally or intellectually ready for it until our thirties or even later, however, so when one loses it prematurely, in childhood and adolescence, through divorce or the sudden early death of a parent, it can leave one fixated on that loss for a lifetime. Because it's premature, it feels unnatural, violent and unnecessary, a permanent, gratuitous wounding, and it leaves one angry at the world, and to provide one's unfocused anger with a proper target, one looks for someone to blame.

No one blamed Sarge, of course, for rejecting joint custody and thereby breaking up our family. Not consciously, anyhow. In fact, back then, at the beginning of the breakup of the family, none of us knew how much we depended on Sarge to preserve our ignorance of the fragility, the very impermanence, of the family. None of us knew that she was helping us postpone our anger and need for blame—blame for the separation and divorce, for the destruction of the family unit, for our lost innocence.

Whenever the girls stepped down from the school bus for their three or four nights' stay at my house, they were clearly, profoundly comforted to see Sarge, her wide grin, her wet black eyes glazed by cataracts, her floppy tail and slipshod, slanted, arthritic gait as she trailed them from the bus stop to the house. Wherever the girls settled in the yard or the house, as long as she didn't have to climb the narrow attic stairs to be with them, Sarge lay watchfully beside them, as if guarding them from a danger whose existence Louise and I had not yet acknowledged.

Vickie wasn't around all that much, but Sarge was not attached to her in the same intense way as to the three younger

girls. Sarge pretty much ignored Vickie. From the dog's per-
spective, I think Vickie was a late-arriving, auxiliary member
of the pack, which I hate to admit is how the three younger girls
saw her, too, despite my best efforts to integrate all four daughters into a single family unit. No one admitted this, of course,
but even then, that early in the game, I saw that I was failing to
build a recombinant nuclear family. Vickie was a free radical
and, sadly, would remain one.

Mostly, when the children were at school or up at their
mother's, Sarge slept through her days. Her only waking di-
version, in the absence of the girls, was going for rides in my
car, and I took her everywhere I went, even to my office at the
college, where she slept under my desk while I met my classes.
From dawn to dusk, when the weather turned wintry and snow
was falling, if I was at home and my car parked in the driveway, Sarge's habit, so as not to miss an opportunity for a ride,
was to crawl under the vehicle and sleep there between the rear
wheels until I came out. When I got into the car I'd start the engine and, if the girls were with me, count off the seconds aloud
until, fifteen or twenty seconds into my count, Sarge appeared
at the driver's-side window. Then I'd step out, flip open the
tailgate and lift her into the back. If the girls weren't there I still
counted, but silently. I never got as high as thirty before Sarge
was waiting by the car door.

I don't remember now where we were headed, but this time
all four daughters were in the car together, Vickie in the front

31

passenger's seat, Andrea, Caitlin and Sasha in back. I remember it as a daytime drive, even though, because of Vickie's classes and the younger girls' school hours, it was unusual for all four to be in the car at the same time during the day. Maybe it was a Saturday or Sunday; maybe we were going ice-skating at one of the local ponds. It was a bright, cloudless, cold afternoon, I remember that, and there was no snow on the ground just then, which suggests a deep freeze following the usual January thaw. We must have been five or six months into the separation and divorce, which would not be final until the following August.

Piling into the car, all four of the girls were in a silly mood, singing along to a popular Bee Gees disco song, "More Than a Woman," singing in perfect mocking harmony and substituting lines like "bald-headed woman" for "more than a woman," and breaking each other up, even the youngest, Andrea, who would have just turned seven then. I can't say I was distracted. I was simply happy, happy to see my daughters goofing off together, and was grinning at the four of them as they sang, my gaze turning from one bright face to another, when I realized that I had counted all the way to sixty and was still counting. That far into it, I didn't make the connection between the count and lifting Sarge into the back of the station wagon. I simply stopped counting, put the car in reverse and started to back out of the driveway.

There was a thump and a bump. The girls stopped singing. No one said a word. I hit the brake, put the car in park and shut off the motor. I lay my forehead against the steering wheel rim.

All four daughters began to wail. It was a primeval, keening, utterly female wail. Their voices rose in pitch and volume and became almost operatic, as if for years they had been waiting for this moment to arrive, when they could at last give voice together to a lifetime's accumulated pain and suffering. A terrible, almost unthinkable thing had happened. Their father had slain a permanent member of the family. We all knew it the second we heard the thump and felt the bump. But the girls knew something more. Instinctively, they understood the linkage between this moment, with Sarge dead beneath the wheels of my car, and my decision the previous summer to leave my wife. My reasons for that decision, my particular forms of pain and suffering, my years of humiliation and sense of having been too compromised in too many ways ever to respect myself again unless I left my wife, none of that mattered to my daughters, even to Vickie, who, as much as the other three, needed the primal family unit with two loving parents in residence together, needed it to remain intact and to continue into her adult life, holding and sustaining her and her sisters, nurturing them, and more than anything else, protecting them from bad things.

When the wailing finally subsided and came to a gradual end, and I had apologized so sincerely and repeatedly that the girls had begun to comfort me instead of letting me comfort them, telling me that Sarge must have died before I hit her with the car or she would have come out from under it in plenty of time, we left the car and wrapped Sarge's body in an old blanket. I carried her body and the girls carried several of her favorite toys and her food dish to the far corner of the backyard and laid her and her favorite things down beneath a leafless old maple tree. I told the girls that they could always come to this tree and stand over Sarge's grave and remember her love for them and their love for her.

While I went to the garage for a shovel and pick, the girls stood over Sarge's body as if to protect it from desecration. When I returned, Vickie said, "The ground's frozen, you know, Dad."

"That's why I brought the pick," I said, but the truth is I had forgotten that the ground was as hard as pavement, and she knew it. They all knew it. I was practically weeping by now, confused and frightened by the tidal welter of emotions rising in my chest and taking me completely over. As the girls calmed and seemed to grow increasingly focused on the task at hand, I spun out of control. I threw the shovel down beneath the maple tree and started slamming the pick against the ground, whacking the sere, rock-hard sod with fury. The blade clanged in the cold morning air and bounced off the ground, and the girls, frightened by my wild, gasping swings, backed away from me, as if watching their father avenge a crime they had not witnessed, delivering a punishment that exceeded the crime to a terrible degree.

I only glimpsed this and was further maddened by it and turned my back to them so I couldn't see their fear and disapproval, and I slammed the steel against the ground with increasing force, again and again, until finally I was out of breath and the nerves of my hands were vibrating painfully from the blows. I stopped attacking the ground at last, and as my head cleared, I remembered the girls, and I slowly turned to say something to them, something that would somehow gather them in and dilute their grief-stricken fears. I didn't know what to say, but something would come to me; it always did.

But the girls were gone. I looked across the yard, past the rusting swing set toward the house, and saw the four of them disappear one by one between the house and the garage, Vickie in the lead, then Sasha holding Andrea's hand, and Caitlin. A few seconds later, they reappeared on the far side of the house, walking up the lane toward the home of my ex-wife. Now Vickie was holding Andrea's hand in one of hers and Caitlin's in the other, and Sasha, the eldest of my ex-wife's three daughters, was in the lead.

That's more or less the whole story, except to mention that when the girls were finally out of sight, Scooter, my black cat, strolled from the bushes alongside the brook that marked the edge of the yard, where he had probably been hunting voles and ground-feeding chickadees. He made his way across the yard to where I stood, passed by me and sat next to Sarge's stiffening body. The blanket around her body had been blown back by the breeze. The cold wind riffled her dense white fur. Her sightless eyes were dry and opaque, and her gray tongue lolled from her open mouth as if stopped in the middle of a yawn. She looked like game, a wild animal killed for her coat or her flesh, and not a permanent member of the family.

I drove the body of the dog to the veterinarian's, where she was cremated, and carried the ashes in a ceramic jar back to my house and placed the jar on the fireplace mantle, thinking that in the spring, when the ground thawed, the girls and I would bury the ashes down by the maple tree by the brook. But that never happened. The girls did not want to talk about Sarge. They did not spend as much time at my house anymore as they had before Sarge died. Vickie moved in with her boyfriend in town. By spring the other girls stayed overnight at my house every other weekend only, and by summer, when they went off to camp in the White Mountains, not at all, and I saw them that summer only once, when I drove up to Camp Abenaki on Parents' Weekend. I emptied the jar with Sarge's ashes into the brook alone one afternoon in May. The following year I was offered a tenure-track position at a major university in New Jersey, and given my age and stage of career, I felt obliged to accept it. I sold my little house down the lane from my ex-wife's home. From then on the girls visited me and their old cat, Scooter, when they could, which was once a month for a weekend during the school year and for the week before summer camp began.

CHRISTMAS PARTY

Harold Bilodeau's ex-wife, Sheila, remarried, but Harold did not, and though he told people there was a woman down in Saratoga Springs he was seeing on the occasional weekend, he was not. Their divorce had been, as they say, amicable. She'd had an affair and fallen in love with Bud Lincoln, one of Harold's friends and their Hurricane Road neighbor, and Harold had soon realized there was no way he could prevail against it.

"I guess love happens," Harold told folks, and shrugged. "Can't fight it."

"We married too young, Harold and me. Right out of high school, practically, for God's sake," Sheila explained.

People in Keene understood romance and forgave Sheila, and they respected Harold for his quiet acceptance of his wife's love for another man. Keene is a village in the Adirondack Mountains in northern New York with barely a thousand year-round residents, most of whom keep careful track of the births, deaths, marriages and divorces that occur among them. They monitor remarriage, too, especially when both parties are longtime residents of the town and continue after the dissolution of their previous marriages to live there, as both Harold and Sheila Bilodeau had done. Bud Lincoln had not been previously married and lived in his parents' house, but until he took up with Harold's wife he had been regarded in town as a "good catch," so people watched him anyway.

After the divorce, Harold got a bank loan and bought out Sheila's interest in their double-wide and lived in it alone with their three dogs and two cats, all mixed-breed rescues from the North Country Animal Shelter, the half-dozen chickens, and the Angora goat.

That was three years ago, and Sheila and Bud had been married now for two of those years. While the two men were no longer close friends, they frequently ran into each other at the post office or gassing their trucks at Stewart's or grabbing coffee to go at the Noon Mark Diner, and there appeared to be no lingering hard feelings on Harold's part. Harold seldom saw Sheila in town, but when he did she was friendly and full of chat, and he, in his taciturn way, reciprocated.

Bud Lincoln was a building contractor, and he had built for Sheila a splendid three-bedroom, solar-heated house with mountain views up on Irish Hill. In spite of how friendly everyone was since the divorce, Harold was not surprised when back in October he wasn't invited to Sheila and Bud's housewarming party. In fact he was almost grateful not to be invited. It meant he didn't have to decide whether to attend or stay home.

But when in mid-December he opened a printed invitation to Sheila and Bud's Christmas party, he was surprised and almost displeased. It meant he'd have to admit to himself that the divorce and Sheila's remarriage still stung his heart, and he'd have to invent an excuse for declining the invitation, or else he'd have to test his ongoing pain against the new reality and attend the party. He'd have to act like an old family friend or a distant cousin, someone more than merely a neighbor and less than a cuckolded, abandoned ex-husband.

"Help us decorate our tree!" the invitation said. "Bring a decoration!" The return address listed them as Sheila & Bud Lincoln. So she had taken Bud's last name, just as she had once taken Harold's.

Sheila and Bud Lincoln had built their new high-tech log house expressly to establish and celebrate their marriage. It was more than a fresh start; it was a repudiation of the past. Her past, especially. The new house turned a simple case of adultery and divorce into a story about finding true love. Sheila's decade-long, childless life with Harold was now a closed book.

Nor was the divorce itself a part of Sheila and Bud's story either. Otherwise they wouldn't have stayed in Keene and built their fancy new house on Irish Hill, barely three miles from

Harold's place. They wouldn't have adopted a baby from Ethiopia, big news in an otherwise all-white, all-American small town. And they wouldn't have invited Harold to their Christmas party, which they hoped to make an annual event. That was her story. And Bud's.

To Harold, however, Sheila was the past that wouldn't stop bleeding into his present and, as far as he could see, his future too. Nearly every night, alone in the queen-sized waterbed they'd once shared, she appeared in his dreams, looking the same as when they went to Montreal on their honeymoon, a smiling blond swirl of a girl who adored him for his quiet, stoical ways. Now every morning, before heading to the garage for his truck, when he fed the dogs and cats, the chickens and the goat—creatures they'd acquired at her urging, not his, and which she, not he, had fed and cared for—he had visions of Sheila setting out the pans, casting the corn, filling the bins, gathering eggs in the morning sun with her long, tanned hands, and he ached all over again with the pain of knowing that she'd wanted the animals because she couldn't get pregnant.

They tried every possible solution, from old wives' folk remedies to in vitro fertilization. Nothing worked. He even went through the embarrassment of having his sperm counted. No problem there, apparently, which relieved him somewhat, but only because it narrowed the potential solutions to the overall problem by 50 percent.

It did not relieve Sheila, however. She could no longer blame Harold's body. She had to blame her own. One by one, month after month, she ticked off the list all the possible causes of her body's inability to conceive a child: ovarian cysts, pelvic infection, blocked fallopian tubes. None of these. Until finally, after being examined by a female gynecologist at St. Mary's Hospital in Troy, she learned that her uterus was scarred from endometriosis, caused by a burst appendix when she was fifteen. The chances of her ever conceiving were pretty much nil.

By now sex with Harold had become a self-conscious chore for both of them, an obligation with a defunct purpose. They ceased making love altogether. Then one spring afternoon, while Harold was down in the valley excavating the foundation for the new Keene firehouse, Bud Lincoln dropped by their place to borrow Harold's backhoe for one of his jobs, and Sheila had sex with Bud for the first time.

The affair intensified and continued for nearly a year, and on a cold dark February night Harold found himself drinking late and alone up at Baxter Mountain Tavern, idly watching a Rangers game that wasn't carried by his home satellite service. Harold had played serious hockey in high school and rarely missed a televised Rangers game. One of Bud Lincoln's old girlfriends, Sally Hart, was tending bar that night. There were no other customers, and the owner, Dave Deyo, had gone home early, so Sally shut off the outside lights and poured herself a rum and Coke and took a stool at the bar next to Harold.

41

The subject of Sally Hart's ex-boyfriend came up. Harold said, "What's with ol' Bud, anyhow? I haven't seen him up here in months. He avoiding me? Or you?" he said and laughed to show he wasn't serious.

In the two years since Sally and Bud had split up, she had gone through two subsequent boyfriends and was five months pregnant by the third, whom she planned to marry. So nope, Bud wasn't avoiding her. "Me and him are still pals. You, though," she said, "different story there, Harold."

"What do you mean, 'different story'?"

She hesitated, then said, "Look, honey, I hate to be the one to say it, but somebody's got to. When you leave here, I'm supposed to text Bud so he knows you're on your way home."

"Why?"

She exhaled loudly and looked up at the TV. "All my choices always seem to be bad choices." She was silent for a moment. "I don't know. I guess it's so you won't run into him when you get there, Harold."

He didn't say anything. He put down his beer, paid his bill and zipped up his parka. The hockey game was almost over. The Rangers were down three. When he got to the door he turned and said, "You might as well send Bud that text now, Sally. I don't want to run into him any more than he wants to run into me."

When Harold got home Bud was gone. He stood at the open door and told his wife what he had learned at Baxter's.

Sheila sighed and said that she had fallen in love with Bud. And it was more serious than just a love affair. She said she would have his child if she could.

He said, "Sounds like there's no turning back now. Sounds like you're planning a whole different life, Sheila."

She said, "That's right."

She packed a single suitcase and drove her old rusted-out Honda to Bud's apartment in his parents' house down in the valley. Harold did not contest the divorce. A year later Sheila and Bud Lincoln were married.

A LINE OF VEHICLES was parked the length of the long, switch-backing, freshly plowed driveway to Sheila and Bud's house at the broad crest of the hill. Harold pulled his pickup into a cleared spot close to the mailbox, got out and walked slowly up the driveway between two rows of shuddering white pines. It was close to four thirty in the afternoon, and the sun was set-ting behind the mountains. The invitation had said the Christ-mas party was from three to six, so he figured he was not too early, not too late.

As he trudged past the parked cars and pickup trucks he recognized most of them. Nearly everyone at the party would be a friend or at least a neighbor. He never knew what to say to strangers, especially at social events, so was comforted. But he knew that nearly everyone attending the party would be checking out how he and Sheila and Bud behaved together in public, and that annoyed him. Well, let them, he thought. Sheila and Bud didn't invite him to their Christmas party because they wanted a confrontation, and he hadn't accepted their invitation because he was still angry at them. People move on. What's over is over and done with. The past is past. That's what this party is all about, he thought.

At the top of the hill the driveway straightened and led to the two-car garage below the house proper and the wide deck and huge brook-stone fireplace chimney and the soaring glass-fronted living room. Harold stopped for a moment and, breathing hard, took it all in: the snowy meadow, the woodsmoke curling from the chimney, the high-peaked roof and floor-to-ceiling two-story windows facing the mountains. Rose-colored light from the setting sun bounced off the glass front of the house and tinted the field and the snow-draped firs at its edge.

He was looking at Sheila's dream house, the house he knew she had always wanted, which he would never have been able to give her. He was an excavator, that's all. A guy who dug holes for people who were contractors, people like Bud Lincoln, who were smarter and better educated than he was, who knew how to negotiate and estimate cost and profit, who could talk easily to people and turn them from strangers into clients. All Harold Bilodeau knew was how to run machines that dug foundations and trenches. He had started out in high school buying a used lawn mower at a yard sale and mowing his neighbor's lawns and shoveling their walks in winter and had gone on to borrow his father's tractor and cut people's fields and meadows and plowed their driveways, and after graduation he had bought a used backhoe and a few years later a ten-year-old bulldozer and flatbed trailer and got the artist Paul Matthews to make him a sign, *Harold Bilodeau, Excavating*. The sign was bright yellow, like a highway sign, and had a black silhouette of a backhoe on it that Harold liked enough to have tattooed onto his left shoulder. At first Sheila thought the tattoo was sexy, but after a while she decided it was ugly and cheap and told him he ought to get it removed, which he was planning on doing when he found out about her and Bud. After that he decided to keep the tattoo.

He walked up the stairs to the front deck and entered the crowded living room through the sliding glass door. At a glance he recognized nearly everyone. People smiled and nodded at him, but their attention was on the Christmas tree in the far corner of the room, a ten-foot-tall blue spruce, heavily decorated and brightly lit.

Harold stood by the door for a moment, trying to get his bearings. Finally he shrugged out of his parka, found a pile of coats behind one of the sofas and dropped it there. He made his way to a long table that had been set up as a bar and asked the pretty kid tending it for a beer.

She said, "Sure, Harold, but you can have whatever you want. They got hard stuff. Eggnog even, with bourbon in it."

He said a Pabst would do fine. The girl worked as a waitress part-time at Baxter's, and he wished he could remember her name, but he didn't know how to ask her for it without seeming like he was hitting on her. She had a tattoo of a thorny rosebush on her arm that disappeared under the sleeve of her black T-shirt and reappeared with a bud at the side of her neck just below her ear. She'd probably like his backhoe if he showed it to her.

Sheila was beside him. She was wearing a red dress with a bow on one shoulder, which reminded Harold of a valentine. She kissed him on the cheek, which surprised him; she had never kissed him on the cheek before, or anyone else that he could remember. She said, "You're almost too late to help decorate the tree. We're practically finished, except for the star at the top. What'd you bring for a decoration?"

"I guess I forgot. I mean, I didn't know." She looked like she was putting on some weight, a bit thicker through the face and shoulders and waist. Or maybe it was the red dress. He felt his chest tighten and his arms grow heavy. She was still beautiful to him, and she was growing older, and he wasn't going to be able to watch it happen, except from a distance.

"It was on the invitation, Harold. We're starting a tradition," she said. "Next Christmas we'll fill a box with all these decorations for people to pick from and take home for their own trees, and we'll put up a whole new set. It's like recycling. Except for the star on top. That stays. It's from Bud's family.

Look, aren't some of these great?" She pointed out carved wooden animals, gingerbread men with M&M for eyes, delicate glass bells and balls, large and small candy canes, chocolate Santa Clauses, plaster angels, and birds with real feathers.

"So where's Bud?" Harold asked, looking around the room.

"Getting a stepladder from the garage. To put up the star."

"Say, by the way, congratulations."

"For . . . ?"

She wasn't looking at him and was about to step away in the direction of a red-faced couple in matching ski jackets who had just come through the door—summer people, he noticed, up for the holidays to ski at Whiteface and go to parties.

"I heard you got a new baby," Harold said. "Adopted a baby. Congratulations."

"He's fabulous! So handsome, and so smart! Oh, there's Bud!" she said, as tall, blond, smiling Bud Lincoln eased his stepladder through the crowd that had gathered around the Christmas tree. He opened the ladder legs and climbed the first three steps awkwardly, carrying in one hand a large, gold-plated, five-pointed star and in the other a plastic cup half filled with eggnog. Sheila left Harold's side and made her way to the ladder, grabbed its sides and steadied it for her husband. A couple of people nearest the tree shouted for Bud to be careful and laughed. Bud laughed back and told them not to worry, he had everything under control.

Harold set his can of beer down on a side table and found

himself edging away from the crowd, backing toward the sliding glass door, and then he was standing outside on the deck, coatless, shivering from the cold, watching Bud slowly reach with the star in hand toward the spindly top of the tree. He lifted the star over the last few limbs and hooked it properly in place, turned and raised his arms in triumph. Everyone applauded. Sheila let go of the ladder and clapped with them.

At that moment, to Harold, she looked very happy. She was proud of her husband, of her fabulous, handsome, smart new baby, of her beautiful house. Proud of her life. There was a light emanating from her face that Harold had never seen before.

It occurred to him that he had left the room and stepped out to the deck because he hoped that Bud would fall from the ladder and the goddamned overloaded Christmas tree would come crashing down with him. He might have broken a leg or an arm. He would have been humiliated. Harold had wanted it to happen, had even expected it. It would have been the perfect ending to his story of betrayal and abandonment, especially if he'd been able to watch it from a safe distance, out here on the deck alone.

It was dark now, except for the cold light of the moon blanketing the snow-covered slope below. Harold knew that no one inside the bright, warm living room could see him out here. He wore only a flannel shirt and fleece vest against the December night. His breath drifted from his mouth like smoke, and he wished he'd grabbed his parka when he left the living room, but there was no way he could retrieve it now without people noticing that he was leaving the party early. People would think that he wasn't over her, that he hadn't moved on in his life, that he was angry at Bud and angry at Sheila, too. And jealous, maybe envious, of their new house and their adopted African baby.

He walked to the north corner of the house, where the deck continued past an adjacent room, a den or maybe a guest bedroom. Like the living room, it was lined with floor-to-ceiling sliding glass doors. When he got there he saw the crib and an overflowing toy chest and animal pictures on the wall and knew that it was the new baby's room. He recognized the babysitter sitting in a rocking chair with an open schoolbook in her lap; she was one of the architect Nils Luderoski's two teenaged daughters, he wasn't sure which. Luderoski must have designed the house, Harold thought. Luderoski was expensive. Harold had never been hired to work on a building he'd designed. The blueprints probably had the word *Nursery* written on this room from the start.

The glass door was unlocked, and when he slid it open he startled the girl. She looked up wide-eyed, then recognized him and cautiously said hi.

"Your dad design this house?" he said and smiled, closing the door behind him, as if finishing the tour.

She nodded yes and put a finger against her lips and tilted her head toward the crib.

He crossed the room to the crib and looked down, expecting the baby to be asleep, but he was wide awake, on his back, looking intently up at a brightly colored mobile suspended from a metal arm clamped to the headboard. He didn't seem at all interested in the man staring down at him. Harold had never seen an African baby before except on television. Sheila was right, her new baby was very handsome. Harold reached down and slid his hands under the baby's body and lifted him gently from the crib.

The Luderoski girl said, "Better not do that, Mr. Bilodeau." She put her book on the side table and stood up and walked toward him, her hands extended to take the baby from him. "Mrs. Lincoln wants him to sleep. He has trouble falling asleep."

They were singing Christmas carols in the living room now. He could hear the slow, muted strains of thirty or forty adults singing "Little Town of Bethlehem." Holding the baby close to his chest, he turned away from the girl and moved toward the glass door. "What's his name?"

"They're calling him Menelik. The name he had in the orphanage. In Ethiopia," she said. "Better give him to me now, Mr. Bilodeau."

Harold held the baby in the crook of his right arm. With his free hand he grabbed the blanket from the end of the crib. He carefully wrapped it around the baby, leaving only his shining face exposed. As if he were used to being held by strangers, the baby stared up at the man, unafraid and incurious.

"Hello, Menelik," the man said.

From behind him, her voice rising in fear, the girl said, "He needs to go back in his crib."

Harold slid the outer door open, and cold air and darkness rushed into the room.

"What are you doing?" the girl said. Moving quickly, she placed herself between Harold and the open door and grabbed the baby away from him. "You better go back outside," she said. She stood facing him with the baby in her arms, and he stepped around her onto the deck, and she drew the door shut behind him. He heard the click of the lock.

He walked slowly around to the front of the house, opened the door there, and entered the living room as if he had never left it. No one seemed to notice his return any more than they had noticed his departure. They were all standing around the beautifully decorated Christmas tree singing "Silent Night."

He walked over to the bar and asked the girl with the tattoo for another beer. She flashed him a smile and fished a can of Pabst from the cooler and passed it to him. She wished him a merry Christmas.

He said, "Same to you." He took a slow sip of the cold beer. "I forgot to bring something for the tree."

She said, "That's okay. They got more than enough."

"Tell me your name," Harold said. "I know it, but I forgot."

TRANSPLANT

The crushed gravel footpath wound uphill from the parking lot through a grove of poplar trees. From the passenger's seat of the van, Howard spotted the monument at the top of the hill—a head-high granite pylon that marked the site of a Puritan massacre of a band of Narragansett Indians. He made out the slender figure of a woman standing next to the pylon. She wore jeans and a bright yellow nylon poncho with the hood up. He turned to the woman in the driver's seat and said, "I don't know, Betty. It's farther than I usually walk, you know."

"Can't turn back now," she said. She reached across him and opened his door and handed his cane to him. "It's not so far. She's waiting for you."

"Maybe you could go up and bring her down here instead."

"Maybe you could pretend she doesn't exist and go sit on the porch at the house like an invalid and watch the sun set over the harbor. You need the exercise, Howard. Besides, you set this up. This is your deal."

"No, it's Dr. Horowitz's deal," he said. He grabbed his cane and eased himself from the van. The whole thing is crazy, he thought. I *am* an invalid. I need to be left alone. This woman shouldn't bring her troubles to me, I've got enough of my own. He stood unsteadily for a few seconds, then squared his shoulders and slowly made his way up the path toward the woman in the yellow poncho.

THIS WAS NOT HOW he had expected the day to play out. Around ten that morning Betty had entered his bedroom without knocking, as usual, and had drawn back the curtains and let sunlight flood the room. From his bed Howard saw the sloping meadow below and then the harbor and the long, low peninsula on the far side, the white steeple of the church and the colonial-era waterside houses and docks of the fishing village, and his irritation, as usual, passed.

"Let's check the vitals," Betty said. "See if you're ready for a walk in the park today. Doctor's orders." She pushed up his pajama sleeve and began taking his blood pressure. She was an abrupt, pink, square-faced woman with graying, straw-colored hair cut in a pageboy with Prince Valiant bangs. Her hair looked ridiculous to Howard. She was in her mid-forties, a few years younger than he. After some initial difficulty, they had become friends. Her short, athletic body was attractive, but in a masculine way that was not sexy to him, and he was glad of that. Relieved, is more like it.

Betty treated him as if he were an adolescent boy, but he felt like a very old man locked in an even older man's body. He liked her crisp, no-nonsense personality and her bark of a laugh when he resisted her attempts to get him up and moving or make him follow his strict diet, drink eight glasses of water a day, walk in the house without a cane. A certain degree of irritation gave him pleasure. Her refusal to treat him the way he felt, along with the daily sight of the harbor and the marina and town on the other side of it, cheered him. Very little else cheered him, however.

"You got a phone call to make," she said and stuck the thermometer under his tongue. "Dr. Anthea Horowitz wants to talk to you. What kind of name is that anyhow, Anthea? She's Jewish, right?" She pulled out the thermometer, checked it and shook it down. "Ninety-seven point nine. BP is one thirty over seventy-eight. You're still functional, Howard."

"I don't know, Scandinavian, maybe. Could be Jewish, I guess. How many times have you asked me about her name, anyhow? You got a problem with Jewish women doctors? Give me the damned phone," he said.

She passed him the telephone. "Don't forget your morning meds," she said and pointed to the glass of water and plastic cup of pills on the bedside table. "Breakfast in fifteen, mister. More like brunch, actually," she noted and headed for the kitchen.

SINCE HE'D LEFT THE HOSPITAL, every morning had been the same. He knew at once where he was and why, but couldn't remember exactly how he had got there. It wasn't the painkillers—he'd been off them for five weeks almost. It had to be the residue of the anesthesia. They say it takes a month for every hour you're anesthetized before you're normal, and he'd been knocked out for eight and a half hours. He did the math again: it was mid-May; the operation had been January sixth; he wouldn't be clear of the effects of the anesthesia until September.

There were still large blank patches in his memory that shifted locale daily, unpredictably. Every morning when he woke, he remembered suddenly something that the day before he'd been unable to recall—his cell phone number or the name of his daily newspaper. Then an hour or two later he'd notice a batch of new blanks—he couldn't remember the brand of car he owned, his social security number, the name of the mysterious, leafy green vegetable in the refrigerator. The patch over his move in March from the hospital to his ex-mother-in-law's summer house had stayed, however, week after week, month after month. He had no memory of the actual event. That worried him.

Howard knew the facts. He had been told them by his ex-wife, Janice, and her mother, and by his surgeon, Dr. Horowitz, and his nurse, Betty O'Hara, and could pass that information on to anyone who wanted to know why he was living alone in a seaside summer cottage on Cohasset Harbor. The explanation was simple. He couldn't return to his own house in Troy, New York, because he had undergone the transplant in Boston and had to stay nearby, monitored by Dr. Horowitz and her staff, while recovering from the surgery. Betty tested his blood daily and drove him to Boston weekly to be examined for telltale signs of rejection or infection. His insurance, although it covered Betty's salary, wouldn't pay for an apartment or house in the area. And he was currently unemployed—he had been a publisher's representative, basically a traveling salesman for the northeast region, a job he was no longer capable of holding. He had fallen on hard times, as he liked to say. Luckily, drawing from some half-filled well of residual affection, his ex-wife had talked her mother into giving him the use of her summer house. He knew all that, although he couldn't remember actually moving in, taking up residence.

He had no problem remembering Dr. Horowitz's office number, however. In the last year, while waiting for an available heart, he had called her office hundreds of times, and dozens of times since the surgery. He sat up in bed and dialed and told the receptionist that he was returning a call from Dr. Horowitz. A few seconds later, she came on the line.

"Howard?"

"Yes. Hello."

"How are you feeling this week, Howard?" She sounded tentative to him, less assured than usual. Not a good sign.

"Okay, I guess. No complaints. Why, anything wrong with my tests?"

"No, no, no. Everything's hunky-dory. I'm sorry to bother you. I'm not bothering you, am I? Can you talk?"

"Yeah, sure. What's up, Doc?" If she could say everything was hunky-dory, he could call her Doc.

"Howard, I'm passing on a request. Not a usual request, but one I have to honor. You understand."

"Yeah. Sort of."

"The wife . . . the widow of the man who donated your heart . . . ?"

"My heart."

"Yes. She wants to meet you."

They were both silent for a moment. "Christ. She wants to meet me?"

"Yes."

"Why?"

"I haven't given her your contact information. I can't do that without your permission. I only agreed to convey her request. That's all."

"Why, though? Why does she want to meet me? I don't think . . . I'm not sure I can handle that."

"I understand, Howard. I know you've been depressed. That's not unusual. I can prescribe something for it, you know."

"It's not like the heart's adopted and she's the birth mother."

"It's up to you. It's not all that uncommon, you know."

"What, being depressed after a heart transplant?"

"That, too. But, no, the donor wanting to meet the recipient."

"She's not the donor," he said. All he knew about his heart before it became his was that it had belonged to a twenty-six-year-old man who had died of head injuries suffered in a motorcycle accident. The man, a roofer in New Bedford, had been married, the father of a very young child. And a nonsmoker, Dr. Horowitz had assured him. Howard placed his right hand onto his heart and felt its sturdy beat. It's my heart, damn it! It belongs to Howard Blume, not some poor kid who fell off his motorcycle, hit his head on a curb and died.

He said, "I've got to think about it."

"Of course. She says she'll meet you anywhere you want. She's young, barely twenty-two, and I take it she's alone in the world. Except for her baby boy. My guess is she still hasn't accepted the death of her husband, hasn't found closure. It's not unusual."

"Closure. I don't know the meaning of the word," he said. He was thinking of his divorce from Janice seven years ago, the end of a brief but perfect marriage—a marriage ruined by the affairs and dalliances that had resulted from his refusal to come in off the road and live and work close to home, maybe run a bookstore, turn himself into a domesticated man, a faithful husband because watched, a secure husband because watchful. But he'd spent twenty years on the road before falling in love with Janice, and after marrying her continued sleeping five nights a week away from home. Howard believed that he had married too late, when he was too old to change his ways. He was attractive to women, in spite of being a cold and selfish man, and he had betrayed Janice frequently, and finally Janice had betrayed him back and had fallen in love with one of her lovers, and now she was married to him and had two children with him, and that was that.

When a terrible thing happens, and it's your own damn fault, there's no closure, he thought. Whatever happened, you live with it. Alone, he had endured his three heart attacks and open-heart bypass surgery and a year later the steady deterioration of the organ itself. And now the transplant. All of it somehow the result of his having ruined his marriage to Janice, the one truly good thing that had befallen him. He believed that none of it, the heart attacks, the surgery, the transplant, would have happened if it hadn't been for the divorce. It was a superstition, he knew, but he couldn't let it go.

This young woman, though, had not caused her husband's accident, the terrible thing that had happened to her. It was her husband's fault. Maybe, for her, closure—whatever that meant—*was* possible. "I guess I owe her a lot, right? I mean, she's the one who made the decision to donate his organs."

Dr. Horowitz asked where he would like to meet the woman. Her name was Penny McDonough, she said, from New Bedford, less than an hour's drive from his cottage on Cohasset Harbor.

"I don't want her to come here," he said. "I'll ask Betty where's a good place nearby, someplace she can drive me to. I'll get back to you and set a time," he said. "Tell her that I'm only good for a short visit."

HE NEARED THE MONUMENT at the top of the hill, breathing hard, leaning heavily on his cane, his heart pounding: Whose heart was it, anyhow? Dear God, whose heart is inside me? It was not his own, but it was not someone else's, either. Until this moment Howard had managed not to ask that question. Now, since agreeing to meet this woman, he couldn't stop asking it, and he knew why he had avoided it for so long. There was no answer to the question. None. He was afraid that for the rest of his life he would not be able to say whose heart was keeping him alive.

He walked to the side of the monument where the woman in the yellow poncho stood waiting. She was very slender— fragile-seeming, almost childlike, with small hands and thin, bony wrists. Young enough to be his daughter, he thought. Instead of a woman's purse, she held a green cloth book bag. She had pale skin and large blue eyes and wore no makeup or jewelry that he could see. Short wisps of coppery hair crossed her forehead, and he remembered her name, Penny, and wondered what her real name was. Not Penelope. Probably something Irish, he thought.

"I'm Howard Blume," he said. "I guess you're Penny? Mrs. McDonough, I mean." He extended his right hand, and she gave him hers, cold and half the size of his.

"Yes. Thank you, Mr. Blume, for agreeing to meet with me." She had a flattened South Shore accent. She looked directly at his eyes, but not into them, as if she had met him once long ago and was trying to remember where. "I'm sorry you had to walk all the way up here from the car," she said. "I wasn't sure it was you, or I'd have come down."

"That's okay. I needed the exercise."

She made a tight-lipped smile. "Because of the surgery, yes. Are you all right? I mean . . ."

"Yes, I'm fine," he said, cutting her off. "Listen, this is kind of uncomfortable for me. But I did want to be able to tell you how grateful I am for what you did. I don't know why you wanted to meet me, but that's why I wanted to meet you. To tell you . . . to thank you."

"You don't have to thank me. It's what Steve, my husband, it's what he would have wanted."

"Yeah, well, I guess I should thank him, too." He paused for a moment. "He must've been a good guy. Thoughtful. Right?"

She drew her bag in front of her, as if about to open it. "Yes. I have a favor I'd like to ask you," she said. "May I?"

"Yeah, sure. Why not?"

"I want to listen to your heart. Steve's heart."

"Jesus! Listen to my heart? That's . . . I mean, isn't that a little . . . weird?"

"It would mean a lot to me. More than you can know. Please. Just once, just this one time." She opened the bag and withdrew a black and silver stethoscope and extended it, as if it were an offering.

"I don't know. It feels a little creepy to me. You can understand that, can't you?" Howard looked down the hill toward the car. He didn't want Betty to see this. He didn't want anyone to see this. A few yards beyond the parking lot the narrow road followed the rock-strewn shore. A thickening bank of clouds had blotted out the sun, and an offshore wind had raised a chop in the blue-gray water.

"Please," she said in a low voice. "Please let me do this." She pushed back her hood and laid the curved, rubber-tipped ends of the stethoscope over her shoulders and around her neck.

Howard said nothing. He merely nodded, and she placed the tips into her ears and stepped toward him.

"Will you undo your shirt?"

He pulled his flannel shirt loose of his trousers and unbuttoned it all the way down. Why the hell am I letting her do this? I could just refuse and walk away, he thought. "What about my T-shirt?" he asked. "Want me to lift it up?"

"No," she said firmly. "I don't want to see it."

The chest piece at the end of the stethoscope was the size and shape of a small biscuit, and swiftly, as if she'd rehearsed, the young woman placed it directly over the incision in Howard's chest. Then she closed her eyes and listened. Tears ran down her cheeks. Howard put his arms around her shoulders and drew her closer to him and felt himself shudder and knew that he was weeping, too. Several moments passed, and then the woman removed the tips of the stethoscope from her ears and pressed the left side of her head against Howard's chest. They stood together for a long time, buffeted by the wind off the harbor, holding each other, listening to Howard's heart.

A light rain had started falling. In the parking lot below, Betty walked around the front of the van, checked her watch, and gazed up at the couple. After a few seconds, she walked back to the driver's side, got into the vehicle and continued to wait.

SNOWBIRDS

Finally, after years of weighing her pros against his cons, Isabel and George Pelham agreed to shut down their home in the upstate hamlet of Keene, New York, and spend the five winter months together in a rented condominium in Miami Beach. The condo was a two-bedroom sparsely furnished unit on the twenty-second floor of a high-rise on Biscayne Bay, away from the hotels and nightlife. If they liked the neighborhood and made some friends, they would become snowbirds. For a year. That was as much as George would agree to.

Then, barely a month into that first winter, at the end of his fourth tennis lesson at the Flamingo Park public courts, George dropped to his knees as if he'd won the final at Wimbledon and died of a heart attack. On the recommendation of the young intern who certified his death, Isabel called O'Dell's

Funeral Home and Crematorium from Mount Sinai Medical Center, where the ambulance had delivered George's body. Then she telephoned her best friend, Jane Deane.

Jane was sitting at her desk in her office at High Peaks Country Day School when the call came. She was the guidance counselor at the school and a part-time psychotherapist in a town where, in the absence of full-time jobs, people more often than not had to rely on two part-time jobs, a reliance in Jane's case enforced by her husband Frank's inability to find work of any kind since losing his Adirondack furniture shop six months ago. Her practice was called Peaks & Passes Counseling.

"Jane, George is dead," Isabel announced. "He's gone. He had a heart attack this morning, playing tennis. George is gone, Jane!"

"Oh, my God! Are you okay, honey? Is anyone there with you?" A tall, slender woman with dark, gray-streaked hair cut short, younger than Isabel by a decade, Jane had worked alongside Isabel and George since graduating college, until three years ago when the older couple retired from teaching, Isabel at sixty taking early retirement and George at seventy taking late. Jane liked George, there was nothing about him not to like, but Isabel she loved the way you love an older, wiser sister.

One of the work-study students, a junior girl in a dark green dirndl and hiking boots, clumped through the open door of Jane's office, laid a packet of file folders on the desk, and when Jane waved her away without making eye contact, clumped out in a pout.

"No, I'm alone. Except for the doctor. I don't really know anyone here yet," Isabel said and began to cry.

"I'll come down to Florida, Isabel. I'll take an emergency leave from school and fly right down to help you get through this."

"No, no, you shouldn't do that! I'll be okay. I'll call George's family, his sister and his brothers. They'll come down. Don't you worry about me," she said and broke off in order to cry again.

"I'll cancel everything and be there by tomorrow afternoon," Jane declared.

Isabel gulped air between sentences. She said, "It's just so goddam bizarre, you know? For him to die in Florida, when we only just got here! I was hoping he'd love it here. He was having a tennis lesson. How ridiculous is that? What will I do, Jane? I'm all alone here. I feel lost without him!"

Jane assured her that she wasn't alone, that she had many close friends, and she had George's family members from Connecticut and Cooperstown, who would surely be a comfort to her, and she had Jane and Frank, although she didn't mention that Frank had not been especially fond of George, thought him smug and self-righteous, and while he liked Isabel, he considered her to be Jane's friend, not his.

"George's family. Right. They'll probably blame it on me

for talking him into coming here in the first place. And they'd
be right," she said and went back to crying.

"Don't say that! He would have had a heart attack shoveling snow, for heaven's sake."

TWO HOURS LATER, having selected a simple mahogany urn
for George's ashes at O'Dell's Funeral Home and Crematorium
on the mainland, Isabel drove their five-year-old Subaru Outback onto the nearby lot of Sunshine Chrysler on Northwest
Twelfth and traded it in for a lease on a new dark brown 200S
Chrysler convertible.

The following morning, her best friend, Jane, drove from
Keene to Albany in her slightly older Subaru Outback, parked
the car in the long-term lot and flew to Miami for George Pelham's funeral. She planned on staying with Isabel for three
or four days. Maybe a week. As long as it took to console her
friend and help her with the logistics of sudden widowhood.
The school headmaster, Dr. Costanza, assured Jane that she
could spend all of her accumulated sick days if need be. It
wasn't as if she had classes to meet. Everyone on the faculty and
in town held George and Isabel dearly to their breast, was how
Dr. Costanza put it.

Jane found his manner of speaking, like his bow ties and
argyle sweater vests, faintly amusing, and sometimes when
speaking with him she imitated it. She said she'd reveal her

plans to him as soon as they blossomed and revealed themselves to her.

Though Jane's husband, Frank, had never been close to
the Pelhams—he was what was called a Keene native; the Pelhams, like his wife, were "from away," as local people put it—
he respected Jane's friendship with Isabel and told her to stay
down there in Florida as long as she wanted. He'd be in hunting
camp up on Johns Brook with the guys for the next week anyhow.
Maybe longer if he didn't kill his deer right off. They could pull
in Ryan whatzizname, you know, the Hall kid, to take care of the
dogs.

WHEN ISABEL ARRIVED to meet Jane at the Miami airport in
her Chrysler convertible, top down, Jane was thrown off by the
warm, welcoming smile on her friend's broad, suntanned face.
No grief-stricken tears, no trembling lips. Jane tossed her suitcase onto the backseat, got in and hugged Isabel long and hard,
a consoling hug. Isabel was smaller than Jane, trim, and for a
woman, especially a woman her age, muscular. She wore a white
silk T-shirt and a flouncy pale blue cotton skirt and sandals.

Not exactly funereal, Jane thought. Taking in the new
car, she said, "I like the color, Isabel. I bet it's called something
like 'espresso.' Am I right?" Actually, she did like the color and
hoped she didn't sound sarcastic.

"Ha! It's called 'tungsten metallic.' I wanted 'billet silver metallic,' but this was the only convertible they had on the lot, and I wanted a convertible more. So, listen, do you mind if we pick up George's ashes on the way home? Since we're in Digger O'Dell the Friendly Undertaker's neighborhood."

Jane said no, she didn't mind. Isabel's jaunty tone confused her. "Is his name really Digger O'Dell?"

Isabel laughed. "No, but he is friendly. Maybe too friendly. I think it's Rick. Ricardo O'Dell. He's Latino, despite the name. Argentine, maybe."

While she drove she punched a string of numbers into her cell phone. Steering with one hand and holding the phone to her ear with the other, Isabel cut swiftly—expertly, Jane thought, for someone who never drove in traffic like this—through the snarl of cloverleafs and on- and off-ramps that surrounded the airport. In minutes they were up on Route 112 speeding east toward Biscayne Bay.

Isabel pulled into the sunbaked lot next to the large cinder-block cube that O'Dell's Funeral Home shared with a tire store, and parked. She asked Jane if she'd like to come inside with her. "It's kind of creepy," she said, "but interesting." Rick O'Dell had told her he'd be with a client in the Comfort Room when she arrived, but he'd leave the urn with her husband's cremains in the reception area. She could simply take them. Nothing to sign.

Jane said sure, she had never been in a crematorium before. She felt rushed by Isabel, pushed into doing something

she'd prefer to avoid, but decided to let it go. Isabel was probably experiencing a wave of grief-induced mania. A way of not
succumbing to grief itself. Sometimes that happened after the
death of a spouse.

They entered a darkened, windowless hallway. There was
a plastic folding lawn chair by the door at the far end, and on
the chair a small cardboard carton with a yellow Post-it note
stuck to it. On the note someone had written *Isabel Pelham* in
red Magic Marker ink.

"I'm reasonably certain that the ashes inside that box are
George's, not mine," Isabel said.

"God, I can't tell if you're being morbid or funny."

"Both."

"Let's go. This whole thing is freaking me out a little,"
Jane said and turned to leave.

"Wait. Check that out." Beyond the door was a larger
room, a showroom of some kind, lit by flickering fluorescent
ceiling lights. On a high four-wheeled cart in the middle of the
otherwise empty room was a white casket with its lid up. The
interior of the casket was lined in rolled and pleated white pat-
ent leather. Except for what appeared to be a bowling ball inside an aqua ball bag, the casket was empty. A vacuum cleaner
tank and a length of coiled vacuum hose and extension tubes
lay on the tile floor beside the cart.

"Check that out. Don't you just love Miami?" Isabel whis-
pered. She pulled her iPhone from her purse and snapped four

quick photos of the scene. "It's so fucking surreal here. Everywhere you look. I'm thinking of buying a real camera and taking pictures of everything. Might be a whole new career." They could hear the muffled voice of a man speaking Spanish in the Comfort Room farther down the hall.

"That would be Digger O'Dell, the Friendly Undertaker. Comforting some poor widow in the Comfort Room with his hand on her knee. Or maybe they're in the crematorium. I wonder where that is. Probably the basement."

She made a move to enter the showroom, but Jane grabbed her sleeve and stopped her. Jane said, "Jesus, Isabel, let's go now. You've got what we came for."

Isabel lifted the small cardboard box from the chair and opened it. Inside was a polished mahogany container the approximate size and shape of an old-fashioned milk bottle. "Like it?"

"The urn? Yes, it's . . . tasteful."

Isabel held the container by the neck and examined it slowly. "Hard to imagine all of George coming down to just this. Ashes to ashes, I suppose. He was such a big man, over two hundred pounds. Reduced to a pint or so of ashes. 'Cremains.' Want to take a look?" she said and started to unscrew the black plastic top.

"Jesus, no! Not here. C'mon, Isabel, let's just go now!" Jane said and walked quickly down the hallway to the door, opened it and stepped into the blinding sunlight.

LIKE A REALTOR TRYING to sell her the apartment, Isabel took Jane on what she called The Tour, first the condo and then the public areas of the building, and Jane learned that her newly widowed friend was planning to live alone in Miami Beach in the high-rise condominium on Sunset Harbour Drive with spectacular views of Biscayne Bay and the downtown Miami skyline across the bay. There was a pool in the building and a health club. An attractive marble-floored lobby with an attendant on duty day and night and twenty-four-hour camera surveillance. Isabel demonstrated how from her glass-walled aerie she could watch the glittering cruise ships glide silently out to sea. She could look down from the terrace and observe the seagulls and pelicans from above. She could spy with binoculars on lovers and smugglers and partygoers in their yachts moored at the yacht club adjacent to her building. Which was how she spoke of it, Jane noticed, as *her* building. Previously in their weekly phone conversations she had called it *our* building.

There was something weird going on with Isabel, Jane thought. She was not prepared for her friend's sprightliness or her suddenly fortified willfulness and new enthusiasms. This was not the Isabel she had known for more than half a lifetime, the woman she had come here to console.

Isabel said, "I love that there are so many blacks in the building and that most people in the city speak Spanish. I never realized how sick I was of being surrounded by people who look and sound just like me. I'm going to learn Spanish," she said. "You hear a lot of Haitian Creole, too. I'm becoming a permanent legal resident of Florida," she added. "I'd rather vote here where my vote counts, rather than in New York where I'm just another liberal Democrat. I made an appointment this morning online to get my Florida driver's license."

"Will you live here year-round?"

"I'll probably use the Keene house in the summer months. At least for now."

"I thought you and George planned on eventually moving into that Christian retirement community, the one down in Saratoga Springs. What's it called, Harmony Hills?" They were Episcopalians, the Pelhams, not really churchy, but believers. And do-gooders, as Frank called them. At least George was. For years he had spent his summer vacations building houses for Habitat for Humanity. Isabel was sort of a New Age Christian, Jane thought. Isabel and George were more conventionally religious than Jane, who described herself as a Buddhist, and her husband, Frank, who'd been raised Catholic but pointedly claimed to be an agnostic, as if it were a religion.

Isabel said, "God, no. That place was always George's idea. Not mine. He turned seventy-three last June and planned to check into Harmony Hills before he turned seventy-five. While he could still enjoy it, he used to say."

Jane knew all this, but had never done the math. "Wow. If

he'd lived, you'd only be, what, sixty-four? Awfully young to be living in an old-age home, Isabel."

"No kidding. We had a crisis coming down the road like a sixteen-wheeler. It's not really an old-age home, though. It's called an 'adult community,' with an assisted-living facility and a nursing home attached, so as your body and mind deteriorate you get shuttled from one stage to the next without having to leave the premises until you're dead. So, yeah. Close call."

THE FUNERAL SERVICE was held at All Souls Episcopal Church with a small group in attendance. The urn holding George's ashes was placed on a pedestal in the nave with George's Yale class of 1962 yearbook photograph beside it. George's tennis coach was present, along with the rental agent for their condo and six or eight acquaintances from the building, retired northerners, couples they had intended to get to know better but hadn't quite got around to yet. Otherwise the congregation was made up of George's three siblings and a sprinkling of their spouses, children and grandchildren. And Jane, of course, who sat in the front pew next to Isabel throughout the brief service, after having declined the priest's invitation to say a few words about George, share a few memories, tell a personal anecdote about George's lifelong love of the Adirondack Mountains, which the priest mistakenly called the Appalachian Mountains. Jane was slightly phobic about public speaking. One of George's younger brothers spoke of George's love of the Adirondacks, and one of his nephews reminded the gathering of George's willingness to write recommendation letters to Groton, his alma mater, whenever a male Pelham applied for admission.

Except for Jane, there were no representatives from the High Peaks Country Day School or the town of Keene. Which made sense, Jane said to Isabel when she groused about the absence of mourners from the north. It was an expensive full day's travel each way, and most people up there no doubt assumed that there would be a memorial service in Keene in June or July, after school let out and the summer people who knew George personally had come back from their winter homes and Isabel had returned from her own sojourn here in Miami Beach.

"Yeah, right," Isabel said. "*If* I return to Keene for the summer. And if I decide to hold a memorial service."

AT THE RECEPTION back at the condominium, Isabel set the urn with George's ashes on top of the sideboard in the dining area, then stood next to the urn as if to lend George's authority to her words and announced in public for the first time that she had decided to stay on alone in the condo in Miami Beach for the rest of the winter. "I'll have George's ashes to keep me company," she said. "But only until I take them back to Keene and scatter them from the top of Mount Marcy, which is what he always said he wanted. By then I should be able to live without him beside me any longer."

She added that she planned to use George's life insurance money to buy the condo they'd been renting and from now on she'd winter over here permanently. She was so uncharacteristically firm that no one in George's extended family tried to dissuade her.

After the other mourners had departed, George's family members, who were staying at the Lido on Belle Isle, took the opportunity to go out for Chinese food. They wanted to discuss among themselves George's money, most of which, since he and Isabel were childless, would soon belong to Isabel. George and Isabel had worked as underpaid teachers their entire married lives and between them had built up a million-dollar TIAA-CREF retirement account. But George, his two brothers and his sister were descended from early-twentieth-century owners of mountains of Minnesota iron ore plus several subsidiary steel-dependent industries in Pittsburgh, and George's portion of the family estate was many times the size of his half of their TIAA-CREF account. From the start George had micromanaged both his and Isabel's modest personal finances, so there was reason for the family to fear that their sister-in-law, who as far as they knew had never paid a bill on her own or written a check for more than the weekly groceries, would not be a responsible custodian of her new wealth.

George had taught math and geometry, but Isabel had

taught literature and art history, and the family viewed her as mildly eccentric, possibly artistic. Isabel's background did not reassure them, either. Her parents had owned and operated a small motel in Cedar Rapids, Iowa. A bright only child, she had been a scholarship student at Smith when she met George, who had just taken a teaching position at nearby Deerfield Academy. They hoped that George had had the foresight to establish a trust naming one or all three of his siblings as trustees, a trust that would provide Isabel with a monthly income sufficient to cover her ongoing expenses, while preserving the rest of George's estate for future generations of Pelhams. They wished they had discussed this eventuality with him years ago. But when it came to money, George, like his siblings, was as closemouthed as he was tightfisted, and no one had been willing to broach the subject with him. ·

ISABEL AND JANE, like teenagers, ate standing in front of the open refrigerator, picking with chopsticks from cartons of leftover take-out curried chicken salad and couscous. Afterward, Isabel opened a chilled New Zealand sauvignon blanc, and she and Jane went out onto the balcony, carrying their wineglasses and the bottle. They sat and drank and watched the evening sun slide across the darkening sky. The coin-sized buttery yellow disc, when it slipped behind the skyscrapers and glass and steel office towers on the far side of Biscayne Bay, swiftly turned into a large scarlet fireball.

Isabel said, "Look at how when the sun gets halfway below the horizon you can literally see it move. It's like the way the sand in an hourglass pours faster and faster as it nears the end. I should know why that happens, but I don't. George would've known why. Something to do with optics and geometry, probably."

"Something to do with time," Jane said and refilled her glass from the bottle on the table between them. "So, what will you do now?"

"Interesting how we use 'so' to signal a change of subject. Anyhow, what'll I do now that George's gone?"

"Yes. In your rapidly encroaching old age."

"I'm old, Janey, but not elderly. Not yet, anyhow. George liked to solve problems before they happen. I like to solve them after they happen."

"And now you can do that? Solve your problems after they happen?"

"Right."

"I suppose it's like when Frank needs some R and R he takes his gun or his fishing rods, depending on the season, and heads for camp with his male hunting and fishing buddies, and they tell lies and drink and let their beards grow and don't bathe. When I need R and R, I go down to the monastery in Woodstock and sit zazen for a long weekend."

"No, it's not like that."

"Why not?"

"Because you don't have to choose between them. The huntin' and fishin' boys' camp in the woods versus the monastery with the Buddhists. I had to choose. The Linger Longer Retirement Home for Old People in Saratoga with George versus a condo in Miami Beach with no one. One or the other. Not much of a choice."

"And now you don't have to choose."

"No, now I *can* choose. And I'm choosing a condo in Miami Beach with no one."

"Well, I just meant that Frank and I are different. The way you and George are . . . were different."

"Right. So, Janey, to change the subject, can you stay on for a few days after everyone leaves?" Isabel asked. "I'm going to need help moving George's things into storage, his clothes and personal stuff, things I don't need or want. I'd just as soon keep his family out of it for now. I'd like to sort it out without them hovering over my shoulder. They're not exactly vultures, but they keep mental and computerized inventories of just about everything. Like George did."

Jane said, "I remember how very neat and orderly he was. But I always admired him for that. Not like Frank."

"Right, he was not like Frank. More like you," she said and laughed.

"In some ways, maybe. Are you okay, Isabel? You seem . . . I don't know, like you're holding back your grief. Your loss."

"You mean, am I in what you shrinks call denial? Probably. Down the road I'm sure I'll feel crushed by his absence. I was so used to his presence. But right now the truth is I feel liberated by it. And only a little guilty," she said. "And he didn't suffer. We should all be as lucky."

ISABEL WENT TO BED EARLY—to avoid the company of George's siblings and their spouses and mostly grown children and grandchildren, Jane figured. Despite an arduous and stressful day, Isabel hadn't seemed in the slightest tired. The opposite, in fact.

Instead of heading back to the Lido, where they had booked a string of rooms, the family lingered another half hour at the condo with Jane. It was a very chic hotel, they kept repeating, as if slightly confused and threatened by its stylishness and worried about the cost. They would have preferred to stay over on the mainland in a Marriott or Holiday Inn, but had wanted to take rooms close to their brother's condominium, they said, in case their sister-in-law needed their ongoing comfort and help, which evidently she did not.

When finally they left, Jane washed the glasses and shut out the lights one by one and went into the guest bedroom. She knew that Frank expected her to call tonight, because tomorrow he'd be in camp and out of cell phone range for at least a week. But she did not want to talk with him. She did not want to look at herself and Isabel through her husband's critical eyes. Not tonight, anyhow, when her views of herself and her best friend were so indistinct and shifting. She sat on the bed in the guest room and decided to send him a text. She preferred whenever possible to send texts instead of speaking on the phone—with texts she was more in control of what she said and heard and when she said and heard it. Fewer surprises that way. Jane did not like surprises.

She thumb-typed: *I solve problems before they happen, and u solve them after they happen.* She read the text over three times, then deleted it. She began again and this time wrote: *When I need R & R I go 2 the monastery. When u need R & R u go 2 your man-cave.* She half laughed to herself and deleted this text, too.

She stood and walked to the window and looked out. A half moon hung in the southwest quadrant of the sky. The lights of the city glistened on the rippled black surface of the bay, and the headlights of cars on the arched causeway steadily crossing from the mainland to Miami Beach looked like gold beads sliding down a string. She could understand how the prospect of living out her sixties and then her seventies and maybe even her eighties alone in Miami Beach had excited Isabel. It was a new world, a semitropical, Latin American city where everything worked because it was not in Latin America. A wholly new life awaited her here. After almost forty years of marriage, Isabel, like any woman, had made so many small compromises and concessions to align her view of what was desirable and necessary with her husband's view that she probably didn't know any longer what was desirable and necessary to herself alone. Jane understood how, suddenly cut loose from George's cautious, reticent nature, Isabel might find the idea of living here six months a year exciting, enticing, liberating. Becoming a snowbird was the really big thing, the thing that George himself would never have embraced. He might have been willing to try it out, but only to demonstrate what a bad idea it was.

In many ways it was a young person's city—especially over here in Miami Beach, a chain of barrier islands made glamorous by movies and television, made famous by drugs and violence and illicit wealth and stylish by fashion shoots and art deco architecture. It seemed that every smart, ambitious person under thirty who couldn't get to New York City or Los Angeles came to Miami. And it was also a city where for generations elderly people from the north had come to sit on benches in the park with the sun on their faces, an unread book or newspaper on their laps, while they waited for their breathing to stop. Isabel was not a young person drawn to the glamour, fame and style of Miami Beach, obviously; but neither was she one of those old people waiting to die. Jane stood at the window with her cell phone in her hand and typed: *Isabel in v. rough shape. May need to stay here longer than planned. Call me when back from camp. XX J.* She quickly hit *send*—before she had a chance to hit *delete*.

GEORGE'S FAMILY FLEW BACK to their homes, jobs and schools in New England and upstate New York, and the following day Isabel and Jane turned to packing George's belongings. With the convertible top down and Jane in the passenger's seat, Isabel drove to the OfficeMax on West Avenue and bought a half-dozen banker's boxes plus several larger cartons, packing tape, labels and Magic Markers. On the way back she stopped off at the Public Storage facility on West and Dade and reserved a five-by-ten-foot climate-controlled storage unit. Then the women went for a long lunch at the outdoor bookstore café on Lincoln Road.

When they had ordered lunch, Isabel lifted her water glass and declared, "I'm really glad, Jane, that you of all people can be here with me in Miami Beach. I'm really glad I can share both the work and the pleasures of setting up my new life with you." She extended her glass, and Jane clinked it with hers.

Jane said, "Actually, I came mainly to hold your hand and help you cope with George's death. This is a lot more . . . I don't know, fun, I guess. More than it should be. So it's like a guilty pleasure. You don't need much hand-holding, and you seem to be coping surprisingly well. If I lost Frank . . . ," she said and trailed off. She watched a pair of Rollerbladers, suntanned, hard-bodied men in their twenties, shirtless and hairless in tight shorts and wraparound sunglasses. They darted past the café and swooped like raptors through the shoppers and gawkers strolling along the sidewalk and were gone. "If I lost Frank . . . ," she began again, "well, for one thing, I'd be unable to hold on to the house. We're second-mortgaged to our eyeballs, first to help the girls finish college, now to help them pay off their college loans. The last few years, with the store failing and Frank out of work a lot, it's been mean. At times we've had to live pretty much on my income alone, which ain't much to shout about, believe me. But I guess it's different for you," she said.

"Financially, yes. My little pension from High Peaks Country Day and our joint account at Adirondack Bank should more than cover my living expenses until I go back up to Keene and settle the estate. Something I can't say to anyone, except you, Janey, so don't quote me," she said and lowered her voice, "but knowing that soon I'll be a very wealthy woman has made George's death a lot easier to bear," she said. "Sounds awful. But it's true."

"I thought you loved Frank!" Jane said. "I mean George. I thought you loved George."

Isabel smiled. "Of course I loved him! And I'll miss him terribly. We were married thirty-seven years. And I could concentrate on that, on what I've lost. Maybe I should. Most widows would. Or I could concentrate on what I had, thirty-seven years of companionship, and be thankful. But when you spend your life married to someone and he dies, in a sense you die, too. Unless you choose to be reborn as someone else, as someone unformed. And then it's almost like you get to be an adolescent girl again. And right now, that's how I'm feeling. Like an adolescent girl. Honestly, Janey, I haven't felt this way since I was fifteen!"

"So weren't you guys happily married? I always thought you were happy together. Like me and Frank."

"Well, sure, Janey! A lot like you and Frank. Better keep that in mind, girlfriend," she said and laughed.

JANE WAS TOUCHED by how neatly George had arranged his clothing. She could picture him taking his clothes out of the dryer and carefully folding each item. His socks were rolled and lined up in rows by color, shirts folded and stacked in their drawer by color and fabric, neckties racked in the closet by stripes, patterns and solids, suits, sports jackets and slacks hung by color and material from light to dark, thin to heavy, shoes lined up in pairs on the floor beneath his suits and jackets like the front paws of large mammals, brown first, then black, then sneakers. Even his underwear was folded and stacked for easy access, as in a men's clothing store. "George liked to say he did it so he could dress in the dark if he had to," Isabel said. "But he never had to."

The files that George had shipped down from Keene for the winter, so many that he'd installed a two-drawer cabinet in their bedroom to hold them, now filled four banker's boxes. Isabel said he was a pack rat who carried his pack with him. She'd decide next winter which files to keep and which to shred, she said. Most could go. For now she would hold back only the papers and records she'd need for negotiating the purchase of the condo. She'd close on it in the summer, after George's estate and insurance were settled. To get the paperwork started she had already scanned and e-mailed digital copies of George's death certificate to Ron Briggs, his attorney in Lake Placid, and Tim Lynch, his insurance agent. The reading of George's last will and testament could not occur until Isabel met with Briggs, who had drawn it up and had amended and revised it annually according to George's changing instructions. She did not know what was in her husband's will and had never had much desire to know. It was like his investment portfolio—not really her business—more his hobby or a low-intensity obsession than money management, just something he enjoyed poring over, rearranging and reconfiguring on his computer late at night before coming up to bed.

The two women loaded the boxes into the convertible, filling the trunk and backseat, and drove to the Public Storage building, where they placed George's personal belongings and papers in Unit 1032, clicked the lock and left. The process left Jane feeling dazed and dazzled, inexplicably thrilled, as if she and Isabel had successfully pulled off a crime, a burglary or bank robbery. In the car on the way back to the condo, Jane shouted above the rush of the wind, "We should've put George's ashes in the storage unit with all his stuff! His cremains! Is that really what they're called, 'cremains'?"

"Yeah, according to Digger O'Dell. But you're right! We should put George in storage with his other stuff! The urn's still at the condo, on the sideboard. I completely forgot to pack it."

"We should get him now," Jane said. "The ashes. I mean, it. The urn."

"George."

ISABEL PLACED THE WOODEN URN on the dining room table, drew up a chair and sat down. She slowly unscrewed the top, but did not remove it. "I don't know why, but this is suddenly making me nervous," she said. "It's like this is the last time I'll ever see my husband. Or maybe it's the first time. As if all those years married to him I never truly saw him, and now what I refused to acknowledge is inside this jug."

Jane said that didn't make any sense. There was nothing inside the urn but a half pound of ashes. "Okay, human ashes. George's ashes. But it's inert matter, Isabel. It's not George."

"I know, I know. But since he died, I've been feeling high, almost stoned, more excited by my life than I've felt in years. Maybe ever. I guess that's been obvious. But now all of a sudden, after not giving a good goddamn, I'm almost ashamed for not having acted properly bereft and mournful. Of not even feeling bereft and mournful. And I'm fucking scared, Jane. It's like George, pissed off and vengeful, is trapped inside this wooden jug like an evil genie inside a magic lantern, and by taking off the top I'm freeing him to torment and haunt me."

"You don't have to open it. You can leave the evil genie locked away forever," Jane said and reached for the urn. She grabbed it by the neck, but Isabel held on and pulled back. The cover flipped off, and both women let go at the same instant, and gray and white ashes emptied onto the table. The urn rolled away and fell onto the tile floor.

"Oh, my God!" Jane said. "I'm so sorry!"

Isabel said, "My fault. It was my fault." She pushed her chair back from the table a ways and, still seated, leaned forward and examined the pile of ashes closely. Extending her right hand, she drew her forefinger through the spilled ashes, moving her finger back and forth, spreading the heap across the table, as if searching for a lost ring, some small remnant of her marriage, or an omen that would tell her how to live her life in the future. What she uncovered were six steel buttons, which she gathered one by one into her left hand. "Look!" she said and held them out to Jane.

"What?"

"These are U.S. Navy buttons. At least, I think that's what the anchors signify."

"So?"

"They're not George's. He was never in the Navy. He was a conscientious objector during Vietnam and worked at

McLean, the Boston mental hospital. Then went into teaching. He never wore a military uniform. He never owned anything with buttons like this."

"So this isn't George?"

For a long moment the two women looked at each other in silence. Finally Isabel shook her head and said, "I don't know whether to laugh or cry. I'm actually relieved this isn't George. Of course, it isn't. These ashes aren't anybody!"

"Should we return the ashes to Digger O'Dell, the Friendly Undertaker?" Jane asked. "Or just vacuum them up and when the job is done toss the vacuum cleaner bag down the rubbish chute?" Jane started to laugh, a tight little giggle at first, then larger, long laughs that made it difficult to speak. Isabel joined her, and soon both women were bellowing with laughter, nearly choking with it, tears streaming down their cheeks. The absurdity of it, the ridiculousness, the idiocy of thinking the ashes were not just George's ashes, but were actually him, George Pelham himself, come back to haunt his newly emancipated widow!

When she was finally able to brake and slow her laughter, Jane said, "You realize that somebody out there has your George in a jar. But if we take this jar back to the Digger, if we demand that he exchange it for George, assuming he even knows who he gave George to, what the hell good will it do?"

It was pointless to try to exchange these ashes for George, Isabel said. Pointless, and cruel to whoever actually had George and did not know yet that they did not possess the cremated body of their husband or father. Probably by now George had already been cast from the stern of a boat into the Gulf Stream or scattered across the green waters of Biscayne Bay, Isabel reasoned, or else he was enshrined on a living room altar, surrounded by votive candles, statues of saints and orishas, baby shoes, cowrie shell necklaces and hen's feet. Which would really piss George off. "I'm starting to love thinking the ashes are actually a person. A stranger."

"How do you know these are a man's ashes, though? Someone's husband or father," Jane asked.

"Oh, I can feel it. You can always feel it when a man's in the house. They tend to soak up all the available energy."

"So what are we going to do with them? We can't just vacuum them up and toss the vacuum bag down the chute."

"Why not?"

"Yeah! Why not?"

LATER, THE TWO WOMEN SAT OUT on the terrace sipping white wine, once again watching the sun set behind the Miami skyline. From somewhere inside the apartment, Jane's cell phone rang. "That would be Frank," she said. After waiting half a minute, she sighed, put down her glass and left the terrace to answer it. The phone was in her purse on the bed in the guest room, and she managed to get there before call answering kicked in. It was Frank.

She knew instantly that he was angry, though he tried to hide it. "Glad I caught you," he said. "Thought you and Isabel might be out on the town tonight."

She said no, they were going to stay in and watch a movie. She asked him if he'd killed his deer. She had learned years ago to ask that way, not to ask if he "got" or "shot" a deer. And it was *his* deer, not *a* deer.

He said yes, a 127-pound six-pointer, butchered, wrapped and already in the freezer. "Killed him over on the north side of Baxter with a single shot at fifty yards. So when are you planning to come home?" he asked. It was more a directive than a question.

She said, "Unclear." Which was the truth, she realized as soon as she said it.

"Yeah, well, okay. But that night security job at Whiteface Lodge, it finally came through. I have to start tomorrow at midnight. The house is a mess," he added.

"Well, clean it up, then."

"I won't have time. On account of working the night shift. I was just letting you know in advance, in case you come home tomorrow night. I was hoping you could get back up here soon. Your boss, Dr. Costanza, he's been calling from the school. He left a couple messages asking if you planned on resuming work soon. That's how he put it. I didn't return his call, since I didn't have an answer for him. You want me to call him?"

She said no, she'd take care of that herself. She sat down

on the bed, placed the phone on her lap for a second, then put it back to her ear.

He was in the middle of saying, "So when are you coming back?"

She didn't answer.

Isabel stood in the guest room doorway, wineglass in hand. She looked at Jane with a steady, unblinking gaze and mouthed the words, *Stay as long as you want.*

Jane looked intently back and nodded. She said to her husband, "Frank, I really don't know when I'm coming back."

"That doesn't sound so good. Is it on account of Isabel, or on account of you?"

She hesitated, then answered, "Both."

Frank was silent for a moment. He said, "It's supposed to snow this weekend, according to the Channel Five guy, Tom Messner. Up to a foot. It was minus ten this morning. It's minus five here at the house right now. "

"It was eighty here today, and sunny. It's pretty much like that every day here."

"Wow. Except for hurricane season, right?"

"Yes," she said. "Except for hurricane season." She said she had to go, it was time for the movie. She wished him luck tomorrow at his new job. He thanked her, and they said good-bye to each other and clicked off.

Isabel set her glass on the bedside table and sat down beside Jane and put her arms around her. It was almost a motherly gesture at first, comforting, consoling, the kind of embrace Jane had expected to give to Isabel, not to receive from her. It made Jane believe for a moment that she could be fearless, as fearless as Isabel, that she could be reborn as someone else, as someone unformed, and that, like Isabel, she could become an adolescent girl again. She laid her head on Isabel's shoulder and smelled her perfume mixed with sweat, and a chill like the shadow of a cloud passing below the sun moved over her arms and shoulders, and when the chill had passed, it was as if the sun had emerged from behind the cloud, and a great warmth covered her body.

For a long moment they held their positions, as if each were waiting for the other to decide what they both would do or say next. And when neither woman decided, they both let their arms drop and turned toward the open door and the living room beyond and beyond that the floor-to-ceiling window and the terrace, the bay twenty-two stories below and the city at the far side of the bay and the setting sun bursting scarlet at the horizon like a fireball, painting the ragged gray clouds above the bay with cerise stripes.

For a long while neither woman said anything. Finally Isabel spoke in a voice barely above a whisper. "I would be happy if you stayed here."

"Until?"

"Until you decide what you want."

Jane stood and walked slowly to the door. For a second, she stopped at the door. She knew that tomorrow morning she would leave for home, for Keene, for the wintry north, for her husband, the father of her two grown daughters, her dour companion and the permanent witness to her remaining years. She turned around and looked back at Isabel, who was standing next to the bed, watching her, and realized that she had already said to Isabel everything that needed saying.

BIG DOG

The afternoon of the day the director of the MacArthur Foundation called to tell Erik that he'd won a MacArthur, Erik and Ellen were scheduled to have dinner in Saratoga Springs with four close friends. The director instructed him to keep the news confidential until it was released to the press, but Erik decided to announce it tonight anyhow to Ted and Joan and Sam and Raphael.

Ellen didn't agree. "Don't you think you should wait? Like he asked?"

"Naw, they'll keep it to themselves if I tell them to." He opened the refrigerator and pulled out a cold can of Heineken. "What do you think, Sam's going to announce it at a faculty meeting? Ted'll put it in the paper?"

"No, but they might mention it to someone who would."

"I'll tell them it's strictly confidential. Christ, Ellen, I want to celebrate! This is fucking life-changing!" He cracked open the Heineken and knocked back three quick swallows and wiped his chin with the broad back of his hand. "Damn! A fucking genius grant!" He grinned and slung an arm around Ellen and hugged her with it.

She gently pushed him away as if they were dancing and the music had stopped. She switched on the electric teapot and shook out a teabag and dropped it into a mug. "Why don't you feed the dogs now, so you won't have to do it in the dark before we go out?"

He studied the two Siberian huskies sleeping by the woodstove. "Yeah. Good idea." After a few seconds, while she watched her tea steep, he said, "Why do I think you're slightly displeased by this very good news?"

"No, I'm happy that your life will be changed by this, Erik. Really. It's what you want and deserve. I'm just not so sure I want my life changed by it."

"That's up to you. Nothing in your life has to change if you don't want it to. In my case, however, in a few days, as soon as the press release goes out, it's going to be out of my control."

"Poor guy," she said. "Poor genius," she added, and quickly laughed and touched his forearm with her fingertips. "But you deserve it."

Ellen was not alone in believing that Erik Mann deserved a MacArthur. He was an artist who built elaborate installations the size of suburban living rooms out of American Standard plumbing supplies and kitchen and bathroom fixtures that he bought new in bulk through Spa City Supply in Saratoga Springs. He had taught at Skidmore College for over twenty years and was famous locally. Though his work was little known to the general public and was not collected or exhibited widely in the United States, it was admired by many of his more famous fellow artists and certain respected critics. He was a member of the American Academy of Arts and Letters, had won prizes and fellowships—nothing till now on the scale of a MacArthur, of course—and had an enviable reputation abroad, mostly in Germany and in Japan, where he had recently been given a retrospective in a jumbo-jet hangar at Narita International Airport. The show had boosted his international standing and the prices his work commanded. Because of the scale and theatricality of his installations, however, few of them were ever actually purchased. Nonetheless, whether exhibited or not, their construction from conception to completion was documented, photographed and filmed, with the materials archived at Skidmore's Tang Museum, where the archive itself was regarded by critics and scholars as a major work of art.

The award was for half a million tax-free dollars spread over five years. One did not apply for a MacArthur. A layered network of anonymous recommenders and jurors decided whose life and career was about to be suddenly embellished.

Based in Chicago, the foundation granted barely a dozen fellowships a year, usually to cutting-edge social scientists and
mathematicians, little-known poets, writers of esoteric or ex-
perimental fiction and plays, and scholars tilling fields like the
history of Paleolithic dance or the hermeneutics of hopscotch,
marbles and other children's games, fields too obscure to have a
conventional academic home. They were popularly referred to
as "genius grants."

MacArthurs rarely went to visual artists, and when one
did it was usually to a conceptual artist whose work more
closely resembled theater or dance than something actually
made by human hands in a studio. All the more reason for Erik
to celebrate. He built his outsized bathroom and kitchen installations by hand in a vast, high-ceilinged studio on the first floor
of a mid-nineteenth-century mill. The factory sat on the bank
of the Hudson River in the once-thriving town of Schuylerville,
ten miles east of Saratoga Springs. He had bought the building
for less than a year's salary a decade ago when he was promoted
to senior professor and given tenure. He had renovated the der-
elict mill himself, stripping it back to the brick walls, replacing
the huge windows, jacking and leveling the chestnut-timbered
floors, installing electricity, plumbing and central heat, sand-
ing and varnishing the floors. He viewed the entire renovated
building—the first-floor studio and his and Ellen's living quarters on the second floor and Ellen's weaving studio up on the
third—as perhaps his most ambitious installation. He called

the building "the mother of all installations." By design, the process of constructing this installation was ongoing and endless and, unlike the rest of his work, was without irony. It referred to nothing other than itself.

On their way to Ted and Joan's they stopped at the Wine Boutique in Wilton and bought two bottles of Dom Pérignon. It was snowing in thin, gauzy sheets, slicking the roads slightly, and Ellen reminded Erik that he'd drunk three Heinekens already and told him to slow down. "If it keeps snowing, we may have to spend the night at Ted and Joan's. Especially after champagne and whatever else they serve with dinner. They like to keep your glass filled," she said. "It lets them keep their own filled without anyone noticing, I guess."

"I detect a note of judgment in that. What would your master say?"

"My teacher."

"Right, your teacher." Ellen was a Buddhist, or as she said, a student of Buddhism. Erik was emphatically neither and enjoyed poking her for her devotion to her studies and practice and her *roshi*. Though they'd never married, Erik and Ellen had been together thirty-two years, nearly their entire adult lives. They'd met when they were in their early twenties in New York, when she was a design student at Pratt and he was living on the Lower East Side, the son of a plumber and grandson of a carpenter, a recent graduate of the Boston Museum School inventing himself out of whole cloth as an artist. From the start they were sexually liberated bohemians, and their life together had at times been turbulent and troubled. He had his love affairs and she, in revenge, had hers, but as the years passed it became evident to both that no one else would ever understand and accept them as thoroughly as they understood and accepted each other. They had no children, and the only thing that they periodically quarreled over now was how to train and care for their two female Siberian huskies. Ellen was maternal toward them, but Erik was the alpha in the pack—Ellen's nickname for him was Big Dog.

When they arrived at Ted and Joan's, the other two guests, Sam and Raphael, were already settled on the long, low sofa in front of the fire, drinks in hand. The men had married in June, not long after same-sex marriage was legalized in New York, and were still acting like newlyweds, rarely taking their eyes off one another. Sam liked talking about being married, especially in the company of married heterosexual couples. "Five years of living together, and every morning I wake up and look across the bed, and there's my husband, and it's brand new! But a little déjà vu, too," he explained. "Like, hello? Haven't I been here before?"

In his early fifties with a steel-gray buzz cut and trim, flat-bellied body, Sam looked more like an aging triathlete than a photographer of color landscapes that deliberately evoked the pastoral paintings of the Hudson River School. His photographs were the size of picture windows and sold individually for many thousands of dollars. Erik didn't much care for them, however. He thought them soft, too easy on the eyes.

Sam's husband, Raphael, had recently turned thirty and had been a student of Sam's at Skidmore. He was writing a novel and had been at it since graduation, but thanks to Sam didn't need to earn a living while he wrote it. Tall and slender, he was handsome in a dark, intense way, with a long aquiline face and pale skin and a mahogany mane of curly hair. He was an ostentatiously intelligent young man with a weakness for sarcasm that everyone knew was only a cover for his insecurity. It was not easy being married to a man like Sam, despite—or perhaps because of—his generosity and warmth, the unashamed pleasure he took from his well-tuned athletic body and his undeniable success as an artist and teacher. Ellen often defended Raphael this way.

Erik found Raphael's sarcasm, what he called the young man's smart-ass negativity, irritating, avoided sitting next to him on any occasion and spoke to him only when he had to. "If Raphael was a girl instead of a boy, a female ex-student living with Sam, and living off him, I might add," Erik once pointed out to Ellen, "you women wouldn't cut the kid so much slack."

She had responded that if Raphael actually were an attractive female ex-student and not an attractive gay man, Erik would be interested in her opinions and would think she was witty instead of sarcastic. Erik said he couldn't argue with that.

Ted took their coats, and Joan carried the two bottles of Dom Pérignon to the kitchen. "I better get down the what-chacallits, the flutes," she called back. "What's the occasion, anyhow?"

Ellen said, "I'll let Erik tell you. Though he's not supposed to," she added and followed Joan into the kitchen.

Sam and Raphael and Ted all looked over at Erik, and Joan spun around and returned to the living room still carrying the two unopened bottles of champagne. Ellen waited just inside the kitchen door.

"Well?" Joan said. "Let's hear it, Big Dog." An endearment, coming from her. She liked Erik more than any man she knew, except for Ted, and Erik liked her back. They teased each other playfully and often. She felt warmed by his attention and charmed by it and showed him her pleasure, as if she knew it aroused him sexually. Joan was a certified touch healer, and Erik regarded her work as a self-deceiving hoax, but she didn't seem to care. She had enough faith in the theory and practice of touch healing to treat almost any form of skepticism or disbelief as merely silly and defensive, and Erik's stubborn, insistent materialism amused her—which sometimes led him to exaggerate it. "People have been healing others with the touch of their hands for millennia," she often explained. It was a skill that could be taught, even to a man like Erik, who would probably excel as a touch healer, she pointed out, given the strength and sensitivity of his hands. She had offered him free instruction, but he did not take her up on it. She was a good-looking, full-bodied woman with thick red hair, and he knew where that would lead.

Ted handed Erik a glass of red wine, refilled his own and waved him toward the easy chair by the fire next to Raphael. Erik took the rocker in the corner instead, as if to avoid the limelight. No need for it when you're the one everyone wants to hear. He took a sip of his wine and said, "Yeah, it's true, I received some great news today. But you got to promise you won't say a word about it to anyone else. Not till they release it to the press."

"The press?" Ted said. "Excuse me? That's me, for Christ's sake! Are you releasing this great news right now, man? Or is it strictly off the record?"

"It's off the fucking record, Ted! That's what I'm saying. Otherwise I'll stop right here and let you read about it in *The New York Times* next week."

"Of course, it's off the record, Erik," Joan said. "Please! Teddy has great . . . what? Journalistic integrity!"

Erik wondered if she was already a little drunk. He knew that Ted and Joan had a drinking problem, but suspected that he had a drinking problem himself, so he ignored theirs in order to ignore his and left the gossip and expressions of concern to others.

Ted and Joan were Erik's and Ellen's oldest friends in Saratoga Springs. They had two grown children each from their first marriages and a handful of grandchildren whose framed portraits and summer camp and holiday photographs were all over the house, on walls, shelves, and on top of the Steinway where late at night Ted played Chopin, badly, usually a little drunk. Ted had begun as a reporter for the local newspaper, *The Saratogian,* the year Erik was hired at Skidmore and rose steadily to become its publisher and owner. He and Joan had a more than casual interest in the arts. They owned two of Ellen's woven wall hangings, for which they had yet to find a proper wall, and three of Sam's landscapes, one of which, *Moonrise over Lake George,* hung in the living room opposite the fireplace. Ted had twice brought up the subject of buying one of Erik's installations and donating it to the permanent collection at the Tang, but because of space restrictions it could only be exhibited when there was no other show up, so Erik was reluctant to part with it. He wasn't sure Ted was serious anyhow.

"Okay, I got a call today from the MacArthur Foundation," Erik began. "Out of the blue." He recounted his conversation with the director as close to word-for-word as he could remember. No one interrupted him, and by the time he'd finished, their faces were glowing with pleasure, Erik noticed, even Raphael's. Apparently it was cool to have a friend who was a MacArthur. And to judge from Ellen's proud, uplifted gaze, to be a MacArthur's lifelong companion and helpmate was even cooler.

"Wow! That's the most exciting thing I've heard in my life!" Joan exclaimed, and rushed over and kissed him moistly on the mouth.

Sam stood up, crossed the room to Erik's chair. He quickly knelt, took Erik's left hand, and kissed his wedding ring as if it were the pope's. "My first MacArthur," he said, then stood. "Seriously, Erik, congratulations! I'm truly happy for you."

Joan said, "Sam, you are a riot."

"You don't know who the writers are, do you?" Raphael asked. "The usual suspects, I imagine."

Ted said, "No usual suspect here. This time they got it right, man. That's such fucking good news! And richly deserved. The genius grant! Congratulations, man!"

Joan said, "People, the hors d'oeuvres! Don't neglect the puff pastries, they're from Mrs. London's."

"I don't know who any of the other winners are," Erik said to Raphael without looking at him. "All the guy told me was the size of the award. They call it a fellowship, actually, not a genius grant. I'll be able to take a leave of absence for five years."

Ted said, "I thought you really dug teaching."

"I can live without it for five years, believe me," Erik said and laughed. "No faculty meetings! C'mon, Joan, open the champagne and pour!"

She opened one bottle and Ted opened the other, and

both poured. They all drank, even Raphael, who rarely took more than a glass of seltzer water with a wedge of lime, and by the time they moved into the dining room for dinner, they were very loud and seemed very happy.

While Joan carefully transported a ceramic tureen of cold leek and potato soup from the kitchen to the table, Ted poured a decent pinot grigio. When he got to Erik's glass, he paused before pouring and said, "If you don't mind my saying, man, the truth is, you have a kind of forceful openness that attracts grace. I mean it. Attracts grace, not from above, of course, in the religious sense, but like from the fucking universe at large. From the life force, man."

"That's bullshit. I'm just lucky is all."

"No, Ted's right," Joan said. "It's what they call magnetism. Or charisma. You're blessed with it, lovey, and it doesn't come to you just because you're lucky. You have to will it, you have to woo and win it with hard, sustained work and imagination. And talent. Until the world and everything in the world recognizes it in you and honors it. That's what Teddy means by grace. Like with this award."

"Come on, it's a fucking lottery . . . ," Erik began.

Joan said, "Let me finish, lovey. It's not a lottery. You were given the MacArthur Fellowship or grant or whatever, because you deserve it. That's what Teddy means by attracting grace. From the universe, the life force."

Raphael said, "God, next you'll be washing his feet."

Erik said, "No one 'deserves' a MacArthur."

"Here, my dear," Joan said and filled his soup bowl from the tureen. "At least you deserve to be first served." She passed Erik his soup and proceeded to serve the others.

Sam said, "Let me propose a toast," and raised his glass. The others raised theirs. Erik slowly lifted his, too. He didn't know why, but he wasn't happy with the way this was going. He probably should have followed the foundation director's instructions and just not mentioned the award, let them learn about it next week in the *Times*. A MacArthur was supposed to eliminate one's need to compete with one's friends and colleagues and fellow artists, but somehow it was having the opposite effect on Erik.

"To grace! And to the few among us who attract it!" Sam said.

Raphael pursed his lips and lowered his glass a bit. Then he brought it back to his lips and, with the others, drank. He put his glass on the table with emphasis. "It's not really a lottery, you know. The MacArthur. It's not just dumb luck. It's friends of friends and their ex-students and acolytes and protégés who end up on that list. And I'm sorry, Ted, but it's not grace, either. The universe really doesn't give a damn. About Erik or anyone else."

Erik said, "Let's just forget the whole MacArthur thing, can we? It's a wheelbarrow of money, and I didn't have to peddle my ass to get it, so I intend to enjoy it. End of story. And,

Raphael, as far as I know I'm nobody's acolyte or ex-student. All my teachers are dead. And I'm not friends with anybody who picks the winners."

"As far as you know," Raphael said.

Sam said, "Rafe, honey, come on! None of that matters. Those folks who dole out the MacArthurs, they all have loads of friends and ex-students who wouldn't even be considered for one. Ted and Joan are right, the universe, or the life force or whatever they want to call it, has been kind to Erik because he's been able to draw its attention to him and his work."

Rafael rolled his eyes and smiled down at his plate while Ted served the lamb shanks and roasted vegetables and Joan refilled the wineglasses. Ellen had been watching Erik warily, as if she knew he was about to say something he'd regret later. She raised her glass. "Okay, my turn! Here's to good friends and long winter evenings together!"

With a certain intensity, as if relieved, everyone drank, as if thirsty, and everyone ate, as if hungry. They talked politics for a while, local and state—they were all slightly to the left of the current governor, a Democrat—and Ted gave a lengthy plot summary of a new PBS series, an Edwardian historical romance now in its fourth week that none of the others had seen.

There was a lull in the conversation, when suddenly Joan turned to Erik and in a voice shaking with emotion said, "You'll still be friends with us, won't you, Erik? Even though you'll be rich now. And famous."

Erik laughed, as much at the absurdity of her concern as the idea of his being rich and famous, and said, "Yes, I'll always love you and Ted. And I'm not going to be anywhere near as rich and famous as you think. Divide half a million bucks by five, and you come out with a little more than my annual Skidmore salary."

"So you say now," Joan said. "But, Erik, none of us will ever be a MacArthur. None of us will ever be a certified genius." She looked frightened and a little mystified, as if she'd received a threatening phone call. "We're not your peers anymore, Erik. Maybe we never were. None of us is ever going to be rich and famous because of our work and our personal magnetism and so on. They'll never give a MacArthur for touch healing, will they? Or for running a small-town newspaper. Or weaving. Or photography. There's never been a MacArthur given to a photographer, has there, Sam? You'd know."

Sam said, "Actually, there have been a fair number of photographers who've received MacArthurs. There was Uta Barth and An-My Lê a year or two ago. Conceptual photographers, not my cup of tea. And of course Lee Friedlander and Cindy Sherman before that. Not my cups of tea, either."

"But it's for creative work, right? The MacArthur," Ted said. "Or for out-of-the-box scientific research. That's why it'll never go to a newspaper editor or a journalist. Of course, we do have the Pulitzers. I can always hope for a Pulitzer," he said and laughed heartily to show he was only kidding.

Ellen said, "It's possible for a weaver, though. Right? I mean, not saying it's me who deserves one, but if her work is seen as more than just a craft, if it's seen as art, it's possible for a weaver to get a MacArthur. Right?"

Everyone was silent for a moment. Then Joan said, "Right. Of course."

Sam said, "Definitely!"

Ted said, "A hell of a lot more possible than for a journalist or an editor."

Erik didn't say anything. He picked up his wineglass and gently rolled the stem, swirling the wine.

Raphael looked around the table and said, "Okay, people, enough about your chances for fame and fortune. What about mine?"

Ellen said, "Yours?"

"Yes, Ellen. Mine. They give MacArthurs to writers, you know. And I'm a writer, remember?"

Ted started clearing the dinner plates, and Sam stood up to help him. Erik made a move to help, saw the plates were already gone, and slumped back in his chair.

Raphael continued, "Speaking strictly hypothetically, why not? I could be a 'genius.' Erik's peer. Even though no one, not even my husband, has read my novel yet," he said and smiled mischievously at Sam, who stood by the kitchen door, watching his husband back with the same wary eye Ellen kept on hers. After a few seconds, Sam sighed, gave it up and retreated to the kitchen.

"But someday I will finish my novel," Raphael said. "And then, who knows, maybe it'll be published by an obscure avant-garde press in Brooklyn, instead of a big commercial house in Manhattan, and wowie, zowie, in a few years every hot young MFA writing student in the country could be imitating it in their workshops."

Erik shook his head and let himself smile.

"Hey, don't laugh, Erik, it happens! Which would oblige the professors of creative writing to actually read my novel, so they could know what the kids are raving about. And a few of those professors will be MacArthur jurors, and in the interests of impartiality, to fend off oedipal attacks, to look academically hip and tuned in to the literary Street and to protect their own largely ignored, middlebrow work, they'll bypass the obviously more qualified novelists and anoint me with a MacArthur. And then I'll be just like Erik! Then I too can truthfully say, 'As far as I know, I have no friends or friends of friends or ex-professors of my own among the jurors,' and can therefore attribute the award to dumb luck. A lottery ticket bought on a whim and forgotten in a jacket pocket like lint. Or, if I prefer, I can attribute it to my charisma and the grace said charisma attracts from above."

Joan said, "I'll get the dessert from the kitchen," and left the dining room.

Ellen said, "I'll help," and followed, leaving Erik and Raphael alone facing each other across the table. Someone in the kitchen was grinding coffee beans.

Erik reached for the half-emptied third bottle of wine and topped off his glass. "Tell me what the fuck that was all about," he said. He pointed the open end of the bottle at Raphael's glass.

Raphael covered his glass with the flat of his hand. "No more for me, thanks. I'm driving." He yawned and raised his left hand and checked his watch.

Erik said, "Before you have to rush off, tell me what the fuck that was all about."

"What I'm saying is, you're both wrong, you and Ted, and you're both right. It is luck, as you say. But it's also grace attracted to charisma, as Ted thinks. I.e., you are lucky to be charismatic enough to have attracted the attention of bountiful grace, tonight's word for the eyes and ears of the world that surrounds us. Or at least the eyes and ears of the MacArthur Foundation."

"Bullshit. It's about my work. Nothing else."

"You'll agree that the value of any work of art at any given time is in the eye of the beholder. Right?"

"Okay."

"And we're talking here about how to influence that eye

in order to give significant meaning to the work. Your gigantic bathrooms, for instance, and those outsize kitchens, they could be seen as meaningless. Or clichéd. They could be seen as fakery. But obviously they're not. At least not anymore."

"Thanks a lot."

"No, when your installations are perceived by the MacArthur Foundation as works of genius, they can't any longer be perceived as meaningless or clichéd. And thanks to the money and prestige of the award, not perceived as meaningless or clichéd by *The New York Times,* either, or by any of the rest of the media, and thus not by the nation or the world at large. You've seen reputations change overnight, Erik. Now it's your turn. Ten or twelve so-called 'genius grants' a year of half a million bucks each gets people's attention. Changes people's minds. All of a sudden, tonight here in this room, as we have just witnessed, and in a few days all over the world, your enormous bathroom and kitchen appliance installations have acquired great meaning. You have acquired great meaning. Congratulations, Erik. You are about to be interviewed by *The New York Times,* NPR, *PBS NewsHour,* and by Mr. and Mrs. America and all the ships at sea. There's probably already a profile in the works at *The New Yorker* by whatzizname, Peter Schjeldahl, the art critic who up to now has not once reviewed your work in those august pages."

Erik's face had tightened like a fist. "Are you condescending to the MacArthur Foundation? Or to me?"

"I'm not condescending to anyone. I'm 'just sayin',' as the kids say."

They were both silent for a moment, and gradually Erik's expression softened, as if he'd begun to agree with Raphael. "What's happening here, Raphael? How come I'm fair game tonight? Before tonight you wouldn't dare talk to me like this. You might think it, but you wouldn't say it to my face."

"Yes, paradoxical, isn't it? You win a MacArthur, and while the others feel intimidated and threatened by it, diminished by it, even Ellen, I feel sufficiently emboldened to attack you. Well, not attack you. Confront you. It's as if in my eyes the MacArthur, by making you rich and famous, as Joan noticed, has weakened you somehow. But maybe, by the same token, since it's no longer necessary to protect you from the truth, it's also made you in a sense fair game, Erik."

Erik pushed his chair back and stood up. He saw Ellen emerge from the kitchen. She stopped at the far end of the table and stared at him. One by one, the others, Ted, Joan and Sam, followed and bunched together beside and behind her, like a chorus, all of them watching Erik as if he were alone on a darkened stage with a spotlight on him. Raphael, seated at the outer edge of the circle of light, hadn't moved, except to cross his arms nonchalantly over his chest. He turned to one side, away from the others and pointedly away from Erik, as if showing them that he could meet Erik's struck, angry, hurt gaze if he wanted to, but instead had merely elected to look elsewhere, as if giving Erik a moment alone to survey the damage that had been done to him.

Erik said to Raphael, "Goddammit, look at me!"

Slowly Raphael turned in his chair, and expressionless, as if deciding whether or not to take an incoming phone call, he gazed up at Erik.

Erik turned away. He said to Ellen, "Let's go. We're leaving."

"Now?"

"Now!"

Joan said, "It's snowing. Don't you guys want to stay the night and go home in the morning? The guest room's all made up."

Erik said, "We have to let the dogs out."

"They're already out, Erik. They're huskies," Ellen said. "They love the snow."

Erik glared at her.

"You're gonna miss my rhubarb pie and ice cream dessert," Joan said.

"Then we have to let the dogs in," Erik said. "In, out. It doesn't matter, goddammit, we're leaving," he said.

"You're the one who wants to leave," Ellen said and retook her seat next to Raphael. The others stood together in a group at the end of the table.

Ted said to Erik, "C'mon, man, have another glass of wine and chill. Tonight's huge, man. A cognac, maybe?"

"Leave him alone," Joan said to her husband. "He's upset."

Sam said, "Rafe, honey, what'd you say that upset Erik? Do we need a time-out?" he said and laughed nervously.

Raphael turned to Sam and said, "Erik was boiling mad and all conflicted when he got here. It wasn't me who upset him. Erik wants his MacArthur to prove he's a genius but fears it was given to him by mistake. That's all."

Erik said, "Ellen, I'm going home. You can come with me or not, your choice," he said and strode from the dining room.

Ellen said to the others, "I guess it's his party and he can ruin it if he wants to." She pushed her chair back and stood up. To Raphael she said, "You're not wrong about him. But you didn't need to rub his face in it." Then she lowered her head and left the room.

By the time she got to the front hall coat closet, with Ted, Joan and Sam close behind her, Erik had already pulled on his shearling jacket. Sam placed a hand on Erik's shoulder and in a low voice said, "Don't let Rafe spoil anything for you, Erik. Really, it's not personal. It's just . . . I don't know, maybe it's his novel. He works so damned hard on it. But nothing ever satisfies him. He's a perfectionist. So he tears it up and starts over. The frustration makes him seem intolerant sometimes. Or bitter."

Ted said, "For most of us life's too short to be a perfectionist. And too sweet to be bitter. Right, Erik?"

Erik looked back in the direction of the dining room and said nothing.

Ted said, "Hey, listen, man, you drive carefully. And watch for cops. We've all had a few tonight, remember. And congratulations again, man. We are truly happy for you."

Erik nodded, opened the door and stepped outside into the blowing snow.

Ellen gave Joan a quick hug and let Ted and Sam kiss her on the cheek. Then Raphael appeared and leaned forward and kissed her on the cheek, too.

She stood for a second at the open door and watched Erik walk heavily down the path, his tracks traipsing behind in the snow. She seemed to look more at the tracks than at the man making them, as if to see where he had been and not where he was going. Beyond the range of the porch light, his footprints diminished and disappeared in the darkness. They heard the car door open and thump shut.

"I wonder if I should drive," Ellen said.

Sam said, "M'thinks so, m'dear."

"I'm sorry to leave so early," Ellen said. "But it's for the best."

"That's all right," Ted said. "We love Erik the way he is."

Joan said, "He's our Erik, after all."

"And Rafe is our Rafe. And neither one of them is going to change," Sam said and put a loving arm around his husband. He called into the whirling darkness, "Good night, Erik!"

Ted said, "Hey, good night, man!"

Raphael said, "Congratulations, Erik!"

Joan said, "Yes. Good night, Erik. Goodbye, Ellen!"

Ellen stepped down to the walkway and saw that Erik was in the driver's seat and had started the car. The headlights cut pale wedges through the falling snow. She stood watching for a few seconds. Then she slowly turned around and walked back up the steps and through the open door into the house. The others followed her, and Raphael, the last to go inside, closed the door on the falling snow and the night.

BLUE

Ventana steps off the number 33 bus at 103rd Street and Northwest Seventh Avenue in Miami Shores. It's almost 6:00 P.M., and at this time of year the city stays hot and sticky thick till the sun finally sets at 8:00. She walks quickly back along Seventh, nervous about carrying so much cash, thirty-five one-hundred-dollar bills. She doesn't want to pay for the car with a check and then have to wait till the check clears before she can drive it home—no way a used-car dealer who doesn't know her personally will accept a check from a black woman and let her take the goods home before the check clears. She wants the car now, today, so she can drive to work at Aventura tomorrow and for the first time park in the employees' lot and on Sunday after church drive her own damn car, *drive her own damn car,* to the beach at Virginia Key with Gloria and the grandkids.

The credit union closed at four so she took the money—
one hundred dollars a month secretly saved over nearly three
years—out of her account during her lunch break and later in
the American Eagle ladies' room stashed the packet of thirty-
five bills in her brassiere. She wore a high-necked rayon blouse,
even though she knew the day would be hot as Hades and the
air-conditioning in the buses would likely be busted or weak.
The number 33 at seven o'clock in the morning leaving from
her block in Miami Shores to the number 3 in North Miami all
the way out to Aventura Mall and then back again over the same
route in late afternoon, early in the day or late, air conditioner
working or not, it didn't matter, she'd be in a serious sweat just
from walking from the bus stop across the long lot to the entrance of the mall and back. And the day was hot from early to
late, and she did sweat more than if she wore a sleeveless blouse
or T-shirt, but she got through the afternoon with no one at
American Eagle Outfitters knowing about the money she was
carrying and is relieved now to be walking up Seventh and finally arriving at the gate of Sunshine Cars USA with the money
still intact in her bra.

She's forty-seven years old and for twenty-five of those
years has been a legally licensed driver in the state of Florida,
but this will be the first car Ventana has ever owned herself.
Her ex-husband, Gordon, when she was still married to him
leased a new Buick every three years and let her drive it with
him riding in the backseat as if she were his chauffeur; her son,

Gordon Junior, when he went into the Navy bought a new Camaro with his enlistment bonus and parked it in her driveway and let her drive it while he was at sea until he couldn't afford to insure it anymore and had to sell it; and for a few years her daughter, Gloria, owned an old clunker of a van she let Ventana borrow from time to time to help friends move in or out, but then the finance company repossessed it. In all those years Ventana did not have a car of her own. Until today.

Well, she really doesn't own it; she hasn't even picked her car out yet. Most of the vehicles for sale by Sunshine Cars USA are out of her price range, but she knows from reading the listings in the *Miami Herald* that Sunshine Cars USA nonetheless has dozens of what they call pre-owned cars for thirty-five hundred dollars and under: cars with one previous owner, cars with low mileage, cars less than ten years old, cars still shiny and stylish; Tauruses, Avengers, DeVilles, Grand Vitaras, Malibus, Fusions, Cobalts and Monte Carlos. Nearly every day for three years she has stopped on her way to catch the bus in the morning and on her way home at the end of the day and peered through the eight-foot-high iron spiked fence surrounding the lot and checked out the rows of sparkling vehicles for sale. She almost never passed the lot without saying to herself, That Chevrolet wagon looks about right for a woman like me, or, The black Crown Vic is more Gordon's kind of ride, but I could live with it, or, Those SUV type vehicles are ugly, but they safe in an accident. Over the last three years she selected for herself hundreds of pre-owned cars and bought each of them on lay-away, and until the car was actually sold off the lot to some-one else, in her mind it remained hers. It was a trick she played on herself. It's how she managed to accumulate the thirty-five hundred dollars—pretending each month that she was not sav-ing the money, which is hard to do when you're always short of cash at the end of the month. No, she wasn't saving up to buy a car, she told herself, she was making a one-hundred-dollar layaway monthly payment toward her car, that's what, and if she didn't make her payment on time, she pretended the dealer would sell her car to a customer who had the cash in hand, and all the money she paid on it up to now would be wasted and gone. So she made her payment at the credit union, made it on time. Today, finally, Ventana is going to be the customer who has the cash in hand.

The Sunshine Cars USA showroom is a peach-colored concrete bunker, windowless on three sides with a large plate glass window facing the street. The exterior walls of the build-ing and the window are decorated with signs that shout, *We Work With Any Credit Type!* and promise *$1,000 Down—You Ride!* The spiked fence runs behind the showroom from one corner of the building to the other like a corral for a hundred or more used cars, closing off half the block between Ninety-seventh and Ninety-eighth Streets. Every ten feet droops an American flag the size of a bedsheet waiting for an early evening offshore breeze.

Ventana stops in front of the big plate glass window and looks into the dimly lit showroom beyond. A very fat black man in a short-sleeved white guayabera shirt sits behind a desk reading a newspaper. A red-faced white man with a shaved head, wearing a black T-shirt and skinny jeans, talks into his cell phone. Multicolored tattoos swarm up and down his pink arms. Ventana has seen both men many times hanging around the showroom and sometimes strolling through the lot with potential buyers, and though she has never actually spoken with either man, she feels she knows them personally.

She likes the black man. She believes he's more honest than the white man, who is probably the boss, and decides that she will buy her car from the black salesman, give him the commission, when suddenly a woman is standing beside her on the sidewalk. She's a fawn-colored Hispanic girl half Ventana's size and age. Her lips are puffed up from the injections that skinny white and Latina ladies think make them look sexy, but instead make them look like they got popped in the mouth by their bad boyfriend.

The girl smiles broadly as if she's known Ventana since their school days together, although Ventana has never seen her before. She says, "Hi, there, missus. You want to drive away with a nice new car today? Or you still just window-shopping? I see you walk by almost every day, you know. Time you took a car out on a test drive, don't you think?"

"You see me going past?"

"Sure. Ever since I started here I been seeing you. Time to stop lookin', girl, time to start drivin' your new car."

"Not a new car. Used car. Pre-owned car."

"Okay! That's what we got at Sunshine Cars USA, guaranteed pre-owned cars! Certified and warranteed. Not new, okay, but *like* new! What you got in mind, missus? My name's Tatiana, by the way." The girl sticks out her hand.

Ventana shakes the hand gently—it's small and cold. "I'm Ventana. Ventana Robertson. I only live two blocks off Seventh on Ninety-fifth, that's why you been seeing me here before. On account of the bus stop at a hundred and third." She doesn't want the girl to think she's already decided to buy herself a car today and is carrying the cash to do it. She doesn't want to look like an easy sale. And she is hoping the fat black man will come out.

"Okay, Ventana! That's great. Do you own your place on Ninety-fifth, or rent?"

"Own."

"Okay. That's perfect. Married? Live alone?"

"Divorced. Alone."

"Okay, that's wonderful, Ventana. And I know you have a steady job that you go to every morning and come home from every night, because I see you coming and going, and that's very good, the steady job. So what's your price range, Ventana? What can I fit you into today?"

"I'm thinking something like under thirty-five hundred

dollars. But I'll look around on my own for a while, thanks. The price tags, they on the cars?"

"Yes, they sure are! You just go ahead and kick the tires, Ventana. Check over on the far side of the lot, way in the back two rows. We've got a bunch of terrific vehicles right there in your price range. Will you be bringing us a trade?"

"Trade?"

"A car to trade up for the new one."

"No."

"Okay, that's good too. We close at six, Ventana, but I'll be inside if you have any questions or decide you want to take a test drive in one of our excellent vehicles. It's still too hot out here for me. Don't forget, we can work with any kind of credit type. There's all kinds of arrangements for credit readily available through our own financing company. You have a Florida driver's license, right?"

Ventana nods and walks calmly through the open gate into the lot as if she's already bought and paid for her car, although her legs feel wobbly and she's pretty sure she is trembling, but doesn't want to look at her hands to find out. She knows she's scared, but can't name what she is scared of.

Tatiana watches her for a few seconds, wondering if she should follow her, the hell with the heat, then decides the woman isn't really serious yet. She strolls back inside the showroom and reports that the woman is a long-term tire kicker, probably a month or more from signing away her firstborn, which makes the black man chuckle and the white man snort.

The black man checks his watch. "Yeah, well, she only got thirty minutes till we outa here."

Tatiana says, "She'll be back tomorrow. Early, I bet. The girl's decided where she's going to buy, now she just got to figure out what to buy."

"How much she got to spend?" the black man asks.

"She's sayin' three-five. I'll start her at five and work up from there."

"Too low. The '02 DeVille, start her with that. The bronze one. It's listed at nine. Tell her she can drive it home for six. Fifty-nine ninety-nine. Sisters like her, they too old for the Grand Ams but still hot enough to want a Caddy. She got the three-five?"

"Prob'ly."

"Gonna need financing. Forget the fucking Caddy. Go higher."

"For sure."

"Get her into the blue Beemer," the white man says.

VENTANA MAKES HER WAY toward the cars in the far corner of the lot, as instructed. She walks quickly past and deliberately avoids looking at the nearly new cars that she knows she can't afford. She doesn't want her car, when she finds it, to appear shabby and old by comparison, not pre-owned but *used*. Used up.

When she gets to the far corner of the lot and walks past the cars that are supposed to be in her price range, most of them look used up. Rusted, scraped, dinged and dented, they seem ready for the junk heap, just this side of the cars sitting on cinder blocks or sinking into the weeds in the front yards of half the houses in her neighborhood, unsolvable mechanical problems waiting to be solved by the miraculous arrival of a pocketful of cash money from a lottery ticket pay-out, which will never come, and the vehicle will be finally sold for junk.

There is a black 2002 Honda Civic fastback that at first looks good to her, no dents or dings, no rust. The doors are locked, but when she squints against the glare and peers through the driver's side window she can make out the numbers on the odometer—278,519. End of the line, for sure. The sign in the window says, *Retail Price $4950, Special Offer $2950.*

There is a blue 1999 Mercury Grand Marquis with half the teeth in its grille missing, bald tires, torn upholstery, trunk lid dented at the latch so she'll have to tie it closed with wire to keep it from yawning open when she drives it to work. A sign taped to the driver's-side window says, *Retail Price $5950, Special Offer $2950.*

Maybe she should go up a notch in price, she thinks. After

all, even though they call it a "special offer," it's actually just an asking price, a number where negotiations can begin. That's when she spots a light blue 2002 Dodge Neon with a big yellow sign on the windshield that cheerfully yells, *Low Mileage!!!* The retail price is $6,950, and the asking price is $3,950. If she offers $3,000, they might settle on $3,500.

Okay, that's a car to test-drive. But instead of driving just one car, she'll try to find two more, so she can compare three. In very little time she has added a 2002 Hyundai with 87,947 miles, clean body, no dents or rust, good tires, and has found a metallic gray 2002 Ford Taurus that she really prefers over both the Hyundai and the Neon. It's a large four-door sedan with a tan cloth interior, and this car too has a *Low Mileage!!!* sign, including the actual number of miles, 55,549. It's stodgy and boring, the kind of four-door sedan a high school math teacher or a social worker might own, nowhere near as sleek and borderline glamorous as the Neon and the Hyundai. It'll burn more gas than either, for sure. But the respectability and conventionality of the Taurus suit her. And unlike the Neon and the Hyundai, maybe because of its size, it does not feel *used* to Ventana; it feels *pre-owned*. Well cared for. By someone like her.

She takes another slow walk around the vehicle looking for scratches or dents she might have missed on her first pass, but there aren't any to be seen. When she steps away from the Taurus, intending to take another last look at the Neon

and the Hyundai before heading for the showroom, she hears
from behind her the low rattling growl of a large animal and,
turning, sees a gray dog coming toward her at full speed. It's
a thick-bodied pit bull running low to the ground five or more
car lengths away and closing fast, eyes yellow with rage, teeth
bared, growling, not barking, a dog not interested in merely
scaring her and driving her away. It's a guard dog, not a watch-
dog, and it wants to attack her, attack and kill her.

Ventana doesn't like dogs to start with, but this one ter-
rifies her. She scrambles around to the front of the Taurus
and climbs up on the hood and on her hands and knees gets
up onto the roof of the car. The dog skids to a stop beside the
car and circles the vehicle as if looking for a ramp or stairs.
Finding none, it tries climbing onto the hood of the Taurus
as she has done and falls off, which only increases its rage and
determination to get at the woman on the roof of the car, a
terrified and confused woman trying desperately not to panic
and slip and fall off the car to the ground. "Help!" she cries
out. "Somebody help me! Somebody, come get this dog away
from me!"

She remembers that you aren't supposed to show fear
to a dog, that it will only embolden the animal, so she carefully, unsteadily, stands up and folds her arms over her chest
and tries to look unafraid of the beast as it circles the car. She
wishes she had a gun in her purse. A person is legally entitled
to carry a concealed firearm in Florida but she has always said

no way she'll own and carry a gun, a mugger will only turn it against her or use it afterward in the commission of some other crime in which a person gets killed. But now, forget all that liberal crap. Now she truly wishes she had a gun to shoot this dog dead.

She is a long ways from the gate where she came in, but the cars are parked side by side tightly all the way out to the gate so that, jumping from rooftop to rooftop, she might be able to get over to where the Hispanic girl or the black man can hear her cries and call off their vicious dog. She's wearing sneakers, thank the Lord, and has good balance for a woman her age, and it hasn't rained all day and none of the cars appears to have been recently washed, so the metal roofs are not slippery. She slings the strap of her purse over her shoulder and across her chest, tries to calm her pounding heart, counts to ten and jumps from the roof of the Taurus to the roof of the Mercury Grand Marquis next to it.

The dog sees her land safely on the Mercury and snaps at the air in that direction, forgets about climbing onto the Taurus and races to the front of the Grand Marquis, where he leaps scratching and clawing onto the hood. But once again in his frenzy he fails to gain traction and falls off. She decides to keep moving as fast as she can, before she thinks too much about what will happen if she slips and falls or if somehow the dog manages to get onto the hood of one of the cars and then to the roof so that he too can leap from roof to roof in pursuit of her, surely catching her and ripping into her flesh, pulling her to the ground, where he will kill her.

She leaps from the Mercury up and across to a white, high-topped 1999 Jeep Cherokee, from there to a 1997 Ford Expedition, the tallest and widest vehicle in the lot, the safest rooftop, impossible for the dog to get at her up there. She probably should stay there, but she decides to keep moving, to get to the fence and the gate and somehow attract the attention of one of the people who works for Sunshine Cars USA or somebody walking past on the street who will go inside the showroom and get one of the car people to come out and call off this animal.

She leaves the safety of the big Ford Expedition and jumps to the slightly lower roof of a dark blue, sporty 2002 Mazda 626 LX, then onto a red 2005 Kia Sportage. Growling and drooling, the dog follows at ground level, not taking his eyes off her for a second. There is no way she can escape him, except by staying up on top of the cars, moving gradually closer to the high fence via the roofs of the fancier, pricier cars, genuinely pre-owned now, not used, Mercedes Benzes, Cadillacs, Lincolns, and cars from more recent years, 2010, 2011, 2012, with lower mileage advertised in the window signs, 22,000 miles, 19,000, 18,000. As the mileage numbers drop, the price tags rise: *Retail Price $15999, Special Offer $12999; Retail Price $18950, Special Offer $15950.*

Eventually she arrives at the last row before the fence, and from the roof of a metallic silver 2012 Ford Escape spots the gate three car lengths in front of her, chained shut and padlocked. She looks at her watch; it's six twenty, and she remembers that the Hispanic girl said they close at six. She is trapped in here, caged, imprisoned by a vicious, ugly dog that has nothing in its brain but a burning need to kill her solely because she accidentally entered its territory.

It occurs to her that she can call Sunshine Cars USA with her cell phone. She can explain her situation to whoever answers and get him to come back to the salesroom and unlock the chain, swing open the gate, put the dog on a leash and lead him away to wherever his cage is located so she can escape hers. From her perch atop the Ford SUV she can make out the Web site, www.sunshinecarsusa.com, and the phone number for Sunshine Cars USA painted on the big glittering sign atop the cinder block salesroom. She punches in the number and after a half-dozen rings hears the lightly accented voice of the Hispanic girl. "Thank you for calling Sunshine Cars USA. Our hours are nine A.M. till six P.M. Please call back during business hours. Or at the sound of the beep you can leave a message with your number, and we'll call you back as soon as we can. Have a nice day!"

Ventana hears the beep and says to the phone, "You locked me in with the cars by accident, and now your dog has me trapped, and I can't get out on account of the gate is locked. Please, I need someone to come unlock the gate and get this dog away from me. Please come right away! I'm very scared of this dog. Goodbye," she says and clicks off.

In less than two hours it will be dark. Maybe by then the dog will have gotten bored and wandered off or fallen asleep somewhere, and Ventana can climb over the fence and set herself free. She checks out the fence. It's nearly three feet taller than she. The spiked bars are too close together for her to squeeze through. She'll have to climb over the fence, which she is not sure she can do even if she has time to spare. She will first have to get from the rooftop of the Ford Escape down to the ground, run across the six- or eight-foot-wide lane between the Escape and the fence and somehow in a matter of seconds pull herself up and over the fence. It looks impossible. There is no way she can do it without the dog hearing her and racing back from his doghouse or wherever the beast hangs out when he isn't terrorizing humans.

She decides to call 911, but then stops herself. A rescue vehicle from the fire department will have a police escort attached. Things always get complicated when you involve the police. They'll want to know what she's doing inside a locked car lot anyhow. Maybe she hid there after closing time, intending to pop car doors and trunks and steal parts, hubcaps, radios and CD players, planning to throw them over the fence to an accomplice on the street. Didn't expect a guard dog to mess up her plans, did she? Maybe she hid in the lot after closing, intending to break through the back door into the showroom and steal the computers and office machines and any cash they stashed there. Before the police call off the dog and release her from her cage, she'll have to prove her innocence. Which for a black person is never easy in this city. Never easy anywhere. She decides not to call 911.

That leaves her daughter, Gloria, and a small number of other people she knows and trusts—her pastor, a few of her neighbors, even her ex-husband, Gordon, whom she sort of trusts. Her son, Gordon Junior, who is more competent than anyone else she is close to, is stationed in Norfolk, Virginia. Not much he can do to help her. Gordon Senior will probably laugh at her for having put herself in this situation, and Gloria will simply panic and, looking for an excuse, start drinking again. She is too embarrassed to call on Reverend Knight or any of her women friends from the church or from the neighborhood, and she will never call on anyone from work. Although, if she can't get free till nine tomorrow when Sunshine Cars USA opens again, she'll be hours late for work and will have to call American Eagle Outfitters anyhow and explain why she's late.

She thinks of hiding overnight inside one of the cars, sleeping on the backseat, but surely all the cars are locked, and in any case she is not going to climb down there and start checking doors to find out if one has been accidentally left unlocked. The dog will have her by the throat in thirty seconds.

Her best option is to stay where she is until morning. It won't be painful or cause her serious suffering to curl up and lie here overnight on the roof of the Ford Escape and try to doze a little, as long as she doesn't fall asleep and accidentally roll over and tumble off the car onto the ground.

It's almost dark now and the heat of the day has mostly dissipated. She hopes it won't rain. Usually at this time of day clouds come in off the ocean bringing a shower that sometimes turns into a heavy rain that lasts for hours until the clouds get thoroughly wrung out. If that happens she will hate it, but she can endure it.

It's quieter than usual out there in the world beyond the fence. Traffic is light, and no one is on the street—she can see Seventh Avenue all the way north to the bus stop at 103rd and in the opposite direction down to Ninety-fifth Street, where her pink shotgun bungalow is located three doors off Seventh, the windows dark, no one home. The narrow wooden garage she emptied out a week ago and where she planned to shelter her car tonight is shut and still emptied out, unused, waiting. Along Seventh the streetlights suddenly flare to life. The number 33 bus, nearly empty, rumbles past. A police cruiser speeds by in the opposite direction, lights flashing like the Fourth of July.

Using her purse as a pillow, she lies down on her side, facing Ninety-seventh Street. She can't hear the dog's growls anymore or his heavy, wet, open-mouthed breathing and figures either he is lying in the dark nearby trying to trick her into coming down from the roof or he is just making his rounds and will soon come back to make sure that in his brief absence she hasn't tried to climb over the fence. She suddenly realizes that she is exhausted and despite her fear can barely keep her eyes open.

Then her eyes close.

SHE MAY HAVE SLEPT for a few minutes or it might have been a few hours, but when she opens her eyes again it's dark. On the sidewalk just beyond the fence someone in a gray hoodie is jouncing in place, hands deep in his pockets, looking straight at her. He's half hidden in the shadow of the building, beyond the range of the streetlight on Seventh, a slender young black man or maybe a man-size teenage boy, she can't tell.

"Yo, lady, what you doin' up there?"

She says nothing at first. What is she doing up there? Then says, "There's a bad dog won't let me get down. And the gate is locked tight."

She sits up and sees now that he is a teenage boy, but not a boy she knows from the neighborhood. Mostly older folks live in the area, retired people who own their small homes and single parents of grown-up children and grandchildren like this one living in Overtown and Liberty City or out in Miami Gardens and the suburbs. He is younger than his size indicates, no more than thirteen or fourteen, probably visiting his mother or grandmother. He approaches the fence, when suddenly the dog emerges from darkness and rushes it, snarling and snapping through the bars, sending the boy back into the street.

"Whoa! That a bad dog all right!"

Ventana says, "Do me a favor. Go see if there's a watchman or guard in the showroom. They not answering the phone when I try calling, but maybe somebody's on duty there."

The boy walks around to the front of the building and peers through the window into the showroom. Seconds later he returns. "Anybody there, he be sittin' in the dark."

The dog, panting with excitement, has staked out a position between the fence and the Ford Escape—his small yellow eyes, his forehead flat and hard as a shovel and his wide, lipless, tooth-filled mouth controlling both the boy on one side of the fence and Ventana on the other.

"If you got a phone, lady, whyn't you call 911?"

"Be hard to explain to the police how I got in here," she says.

"Yeah, prob'ly would," he says. "How *did* you get in there?"

"Don't matter. Looking for a car to buy. What matters is how am I gonna get out of here?"

They are both silent for a moment. Finally he says, "Maybe somebody with a crane could do it. You know, lower a hook so you could grab onto it and get lifted out?"

She pictures that and says, "No way. I'd end up on the evening news for sure."

"I'm gonna call 911 for you, lady. Don't worry, they'll get you outa there."

"No, don't!" she cries, but it's too late, he already has his cell phone out and is making the call.

A dispatcher answers, and the boy says he's calling to report that there is a lady trapped by a vicious dog inside a car lot on Northwest Seventh and Ninety-seventh Street. "She needs to be rescued," he says.

The dispatcher asks for the name of the car lot, and the boy tells her. She asks his name, and he says Reynaldo Rodriquez. Ventana connects his last name to the tag worn by a hugely fat woman she knows slightly who lives on Ninety-sixth and works the early shift at Esther's Diner on 103rd. You can't tell her age because of the fatness, but she's likely the boy's aunt or older sister, and he's been visiting her. Obviously a nice boy. Like her Gordon Junior at the same age.

She hears Reynaldo tell the dispatcher that he personally doesn't know the lady in the Sunshine Cars USA lot or how she got in there. He says he doesn't think there is a burglar alarm, he doesn't hear one anyhow, all he can see or hear is a lady trapped inside a locked fence by a guard dog. He says she is sitting on the roof of one of the cars to escape the dog. He listens and after a pause asks why should he call the police? The lady isn't doing anything illegal. He listens for a few seconds more, says okay and clicks off.

"Told me the situation not 911's job to decide on. Told me they just a call center, not the police. She said I was calling about a break-in. Told me to call the cops directly," he says to Ventana. "Even gave me the precinct phone number."

"Don't."

"Okay, I won't. Too bad you not a cat in a tree. Fire department be over here in a minute, no questions asked." He leans down and looks the dog in its small eyes, and the dog stares back and growls from somewhere deep in his chest.

She says, "Whyn't you go way over to the other side of the lot on Ninety-eighth? Make a bunch of noise by the fence, like you trying to get in. When the dog runs over to stop you, I'll try to climb over the fence. Let's try that."

"Okay. But I could get busted, y' know, if it look like I'm trying to rob from these cars or break into the building. Which it would. They prob'ly have surveillance cameras. They everywhere, you know."

She agrees. She tells him to forget it, she'll just have to spend the night up here on top of this SUV, hope it doesn't rain, and wait till they open the door of the dealership in the morning.

Reynaldo has his phone out again, has looked up a number and is tapping it in.

"Who you calling now?"

"If you see something, say something, yo. That's what they always telling us, right?"

"Who?"

"The television people. Channel Five News," he says. "I be seeing something, so now I be saying something." And before she has a chance to tell him to stop, he is talking to a producer, telling her there is a lady held prisoner by a vicious mean pit bull inside a locked used-car lot on Northwest Seventh and Ninety-seventh Street. "That's right," he says, "Sunshine Cars USA. And 911, I called them for her myself, and they refused to help her. Re-fused! You should send a camera crew out here right now and put it on the eleven o'clock news, so this lady can get help. Maybe the people who own the used-car dealership will see it on TV and will come unlock the fence and call off their disgusting dog."

The producer asks him who he is, and he gives her his name and says he's a passerby. The woman tells him to wait there for the crew to arrive, because they'd like to tape him too. She says they'll be there in a matter of minutes.

He says he'll wait for them and clicks off. Grinning, he says to Ventana, "We gonna be famous, yo."

"I don't want to be famous. I just want to get free of this dog and his fence and his cars and go home."

"Sometimes being famous the only way to get free," the boy says. "What about Muhammad Ali? Famous. Or O.J.? Remember him? Famous. What about Jay-Z? Famous and free. I could name lots of people."

"Reynaldo, stop," Ventana says. "You're only a child."

"That's okay," he says and laughs. "I still know stuff."

For the next fifteen minutes Ventana and Reynaldo chat as if they are sitting across a table at Esther's Diner, and indeed it turns out that the very large waitress at Esther's whose name tag says Esmeralda Rodriquez is his mother. Reynaldo says he visits his moms once a week but lives with his father and his father's new wife over in Miami Gardens, because supposedly the schools are better there, though he is not all that cool about his father's new wife. Ventana asks why not, and he shrugs and says she is real young and disses his mother to him, which is definitely not cool. Ventana asks why he doesn't talk to his father about it, ask him to make her stop talking bad about his mother. He says they don't have that kind of relationship.

She says, "Oh." Then they go silent for a few moments. She likes the boy, but is not happy that he called the television station. Too late now. And maybe the boy is right, that somehow getting on television will set her free.

A white van with the CBS eye and a large blue 5 painted on the side turns off Seventh Avenue onto Ninety-seventh Street and parks close to where Reynaldo stands on the sidewalk. The driver, a cameraman, and a sound man get out of the van and start removing lights, sound boom, cables, battery, camera and tripod from the back. Behind the van comes a pale green Ford Taurus, a lot like the one Ventana planned to test-drive, driven by a black woman with straightened hair. The tall young woman gets out of the car. She's wearing a leather miniskirt and lavender silk blouse and looks like an actress or a model. Her face shines. She speaks with the cameraman and his crew for a moment, then walks over to Reynaldo. She asks if he is the person who called "See Something Say Something" at Channel 5.

He says yes and points up at Ventana atop the silver Ford Escape. "She the one trapped inside the car lot, though. That dog there, he the one won't let her get down off the car and climb over the fence."

While the reporter touches up her makeup she asks him if it is true that he called 911 and they refused to help, and he says yes. They just told him to call the police in case it was a break-in.

The reporter says, "Was it a break-in?"

He laughs. "A little early in the night for robbing. Whyn't you ask her? Get it on camera," Reynaldo suggests. "You can get me on camera too, y' know. I recognize you from the TV," he says. "Forgot your name, though."

"Autumn Fowler," she says. When the cameraman has his camera set up with the high spiked fence, silver Ford Escape and Ventana clustered in the central background, the reporter steps directly into the central foreground. The soundman swings his boom over her head just out of camera range. The driver, their lighting man, has arranged his lights so he can illuminate Autumn Fowler, Ventana and Reynaldo in turn simply by swinging the reflector disk. By now the dog has moved into the bright circle of light and is bouncing up and down, growling and scowling like a boxer stepping into the ring, demonstrating to the crowd that he will explode with fury against anyone foolish enough to enter the ring with him.

Several people have been hesitantly approaching along the sidewalk and edging up to the van. Others are emerging from nearby houses, and soon a crowd has gathered, drawn like moths to the lights, the camera, the tall, glamorous woman clipping a mic onto her blouse. One by one they realize why the camera, lights and mic and the famous TV reporter have come to their neighborhood—it is the frightened middle-aged woman atop a silver SUV, one of their neighbors, a friend to some of them, and she's trapped inside a chained and locked used-car lot by a pit bull guard dog. Several of them say her name to one another and wonder how on earth Ventana Robertson got herself into this situation. A couple of them speculate that because Ventana's so smart and resourceful it might be she's doing it for a reality TV program.

Autumn Fowler says to the cameraman, "Let me do the intro, then when I point to it pan down to the dog and up to the woman when I point to her. After I ask her a couple questions, come back to me, and then I'll talk to the kid for a minute."

"Gotcha."

"How long will I be on TV?" Reynaldo asks.

Autumn Fowler smiles at him. "Long enough for all your friends to recognize you."

"Awesome."

The reporter calls up to Ventana and asks her name.

Ventana says, "I don't want you to say my name on TV. I just want to get the people who own the dog to come put him on a leash so I can get down from here and go home."

"I understand. I may have to ask you to sign a release. Can you do that? You, too," she says to Reynaldo.

"If you can get me out of here, I'll sign anything," Ventana says.

"Me, too. But you can say my name on TV. It's Reynaldo Rodriquez," he says and spells Reynaldo for her.

"Thank you, Reynaldo."

"No problem, Autumn."

Autumn speaks to the camera for a few seconds, telling the viewers at home who she is and where she's reporting from. She briefly describes Ventana's plight, turns to Ventana and calls out to her, "Can you tell us how you got locked behind the fence, ma'am?"

"I was looking to buy a car. I guess they forgot I was here, the people who own the cars, and they locked the gate and went home. I tried calling . . ."

"And this dog," Autumn says, interrupting her, "this vicious dog has kept you from climbing over the fence and getting out? Is that correct?" she says and signals for the cameraman to start filming the dog, who on cue promptly lunges snarling against the fence.

"Yes, that's correct."

"You have a cell phone, I understand. Did you call 911?"

From behind her Reynaldo says, "I the one called 911. She didn't want me to."

Autumn shakes her head with irritation. "I'll get to you in a minute," she says. Then, to Ventana, "Can you tell our viewers what happened when you called 911?"

"They said it must be a break-in so it wasn't their problem. It was something for the police," Ventana says, adding that she left a message on the used-car dealer's answering machine, but that didn't do any good, either. "They must not be checking their messages. I hope they watch the TV news tonight, so they can come leash up this dog and unlock the gate."

"Otherwise?"

"Otherwise I'll be staying up here till tomorrow morning when they come in to work."

Autumn turns to the camera. "There you have it. A woman alone, forced to sleep outside in the cold damp night like a homeless person, terrorized by a vicious guard dog, locked inside a cage like an animal. And when she calls 911 for help, she's turned away." She signals for the cameraman and lighting and soundman to focus on Reynaldo. "You were the one who called 911 for her, is that correct?" she asks him.

"Yes, ma'am. That is correct. My name is Reynaldo Rod-riquez. From Miami Gardens."

Autumn turns away from him and faces the camera again. "Thank you, Reynaldo. A good Samaritan, a young man who heard something and then said something. Remember, folks, if you hear something, say something. Call us at 305-591-5555 or e-mail us at hearandsay at cbsmiami dot com. This is Autumn Fowler in Miami Shores."

She plucks the mike off her blouse and tells the camera-man she's done.

Reynaldo says, "Don't you want to ask me or the lady there some more questions? Maybe you could call 911 yourself, do it with the camera running. That'd be awesome TV!"

"Sorry, kid. This is sort of a cat stuck in a tree story. Not as big and exciting as you think." She hands him the release to sign. He scrawls his name and gives the form back to her. She calls up to Ventana, "Don't worry about signing the release, hon, since we never used your name." She steps into her car and starts the engine. While the cameraman and his two as-sistants collect their equipment and cables and stash them in the van, she slowly parts the gathered crowd with her car and drives off. A minute later the crew and their van have departed from the scene.

With the lights, camera and famous television reporter gone, the crowd of bystanders quickly loses interest. They're not worried about Ventana: now that she's been filmed for

TV broadcast she's entered a different and higher level of reality and power than theirs. They drift back to their homes and apartments, where they'll wait to watch the late news on Channel 5, hoping to catch a glimpse of themselves in the background, their neighborhood, the used-car dealership they walk past every day of their lives, all of it made more radiant, color-soaked and multidimensional on high-definition TV than it could ever be in real life. The teenage son of their neighbor Esmeralda Rodriquez will be remembered mainly for standing in the way of a clear view of the reporter. The woman trapped behind the fence by the guard dog, their neighbor Ventana Robertson, her face and plight lost in the bright light of television and the presence right here in the neighborhood of the beautiful, charismatic reporter, will be all but forgotten. It's as if an angel unexpectedly landed on Northwest Seventh Avenue and Ninety-seventh Street, and afterward, when the angel flies back to her kingdom in the sky, no one tries to remember the occasion for her visit. They remember only that an angel was briefly here on earth, proving that a higher order of being truly does exist.

"You okay?" Reynaldo says.

"Of course not! I'm still up here, aren't I? That dog's still down there."

Reynaldo is silent for a moment. "Maybe when they show it on the eleven o'clock news . . ."

"You poor child! Not gonna happen. You heard her, this

just a cat up a tree story to her and her TV people. You g'wan home to your daddy's house now. Takes a while to get across town to Miami Gardens by bus, and you prob'ly got a curfew."

He scrapes the toe of his left sneaker against the pavement. Then the right. "You gonna be all right?" '

"Yes! Now git!" She's not angry at him, and in fact she's grateful for his kindness, but nonetheless is shouting angrily at him, "G'wan, now git!"

"Okay, okay, chill. I'm going." He takes a few steps toward Seventh, then turns and says, "Hope it don't rain on you."

"I said git!" she yells, and Reynaldo runs.

VENTANA IS ALONE NOW. Except for the dog. He seems calmer since everyone's left. And he's no longer growling. He's curled up like a thick gray knot of muscle at the front of the Honda van parked beside her SUV and seems to be sleeping. Ventana wishes she knew his name. If she knew his name she could talk to him, maybe reassure him as to her good intentions. He must know already that she means no harm to him and his owner. For over four hours she's been his prisoner and has done nothing to threaten him. In the beginning when she ran from him and climbed up on the roof of the Taurus that she wanted to test-drive and maybe buy and then hopped from roof to roof until ending here on top of the silver Ford Escape, he must have reasoned, assuming guard dogs in some way reason, that she was guilty of a crime or was about to commit one. She probably shouldn't have run like that, should have stood her ground instead, but he terrified her.

But that was a long while ago, and since then she's been his only companion here behind the fence, while on the other side of the fence, people have come and gone, they've stared at him and been scared of him, and have aimed lights and cameras at him for a TV audience. The whole neighborhood has come by and looked at him and her, too, as if they were animals in a zoo. By now he must be used to Ventana's presence, as if they are cage mates, not enemies.

Slowly she hitches her way to the edge of the roof and, more open-minded than before, carefully, calmly, almost objectively, examines the dog. She's still frightened, but the sight of him no longer panics her. He's large for a pit bull, maybe fifty or sixty pounds—she's seen many examples of the breed in the neighborhood walking with that characteristic bow-legged, chesty strut, in the company of young men wearing baggy pants halfway down their underwear, tight muscle shirts and baseball caps on backward, boys who are barely men and resemble their dogs the way people say dogs and their owners and husbands and wives come to resemble each other. She knows some of those young men personally, has known them since they were little boys. Inside they're not hard and dangerous; they're soft and scared. That's why they need to walk the streets with a hard, dangerous-looking dog yanking on a chain-link leash.

She notices that the dog has been watching her with his yellow eyes half opened. He still hasn't moved, except for the rise and fall of his barrel-hooped chest—he's breathing through his nose, with his lipless mouth closed over his teeth like a giant python. A good sign, she thinks. She lets her legs dangle over the windshield of the vehicle, her feet almost touching the hood. The dog doesn't stir.

"What's your name, dog?" She almost laughs at the question. She can call him whatever she wants and that'll be his name, at least for tonight. She wonders if he belongs to the black salesman or the skinny white one. She doesn't know what a tattooed white man would name his guard dog, but if he's owned by the black man his name would be something country and southern, like Blue. She remembers a line from an old song, *I had a dog and his name was Blue . . .*

"Hey, Blue, you gonna let the nice lady come down?"

At the sound of her voice the dog lifts his massive head, looks up at Ventana for a few seconds, then lowers his head again, watching her with eyes wide open now, his small ears tipped forward, his forehead rippled as if with thought. Ventana remembers some more lines from the song and sings them to him. She has a thin, almost reedy singing voice:

You know Blue was a good ol' dog,
Treed a possum in a hollow log.
You know from that he was a good ol' dog . . .

Ol' Blue's feet was big and round,
Never 'lowed a possum to touch the ground . . .

No response from Blue, which she decides is a good sign, so she slides forward, and when her feet touch the hood of the car, she stands up. Feet apart, hands on her hips, shoulders squared, she believes she is the picture of self-confidence and good intentions. "Well, well, Blue," she says, smiling. "What do you make of this? I'm starting to think we're gonna be friends, you and me."

Blue stands, squares his shoulders similarly and appears to smile back. He whips his tail like a piece of steel cable back and forth in a friendly-seeming way and droops his ears in a manner that suggests submission to Ventana, as if he's decided that for the moment, until his owner shows up, she's the boss. Must be his owner is the black man, she thinks, since he's so relaxed around black people. Maybe the white man's not the boss, like she originally thought. She decided earlier that when she got out of here, whether it happened tonight or tomorrow morning, she would not come back and test-drive and buy a vehicle from Sunshine Cars USA. But now she's thinking maybe she will.

She sits down on the hood and tells Blue face-to-face that she's going to walk over to the gate in the fence and try to climb over it. "Sorry to leave you, ol' Blue, but I got to get home," she explains. "I got to work tomorrow, and I need my sleep."

Keeping the silver Ford between them, still not taking her eyes off the dog, she slides her feet from the hood of the car to the ground and takes a short step away from the vehicle. Blue has watched her descent, and except to stand up and flip his tail back and forth has not reacted, has not even blinked. For the first time since she left the roof of the car, she takes her eyes off him—a ten-second trial. When she turns back he has not moved or changed his expression. He's watching her almost as if he's glad she's leaving, as if her departure will relieve him of duty and he'll be free to find a quiet spot in the lot to sleep away the rest of the night.

"Okay, I'm going now," she says. "Goodbye, Blue."

Ventana walks slowly along the fence toward the locked gate three car lengths away. She doesn't look back at Blue, and she doesn't walk tentatively; she walks like someone who is not afraid, faking it the same way she entered the lot hours earlier. She was afraid then, too, but only of buying a car, of being outsmarted by the salesman—or saleswoman, if she ended up buying it from the young Latina. She was afraid that the car would turn out to be a lemon, rusting on cinder blocks in her backyard, used up; that depositing one hundred dollars in the credit union at the end of every month for three long years would be wasted. Now she is afraid that she has dangerously misread a guard dog's intentions and desires. Though she walks with seeming confidence, she may be sacrificing herself to a set of obscure but nonetheless sacred principles of property and commerce. She is afraid of the blinding pain that will come if the guard dog attacks her. And for a second she lets herself imagine the awful relief that will come when only death can take away the pain. Her night has come to that.

She remembers another verse from that old song, but this time sings it silently to herself:

Old Blue died and I dug his grave,
I dug his grave with a silver spade.

The chained and padlocked gate is wide enough to drive a car through if it were open. Just below the top of the eight-foot-tall spikes is a horizontal steel pipe that she believes she is tall enough to reach. She adjusts her purse so the strap crosses her chest and the bag hangs against her back. She reaches up and on tiptoes grabs the pipe. She pulls herself a few inches off the ground, then a few more, until she's high enough to work her right elbow through the spikes and over the pipe. Holding her weight with her upper right arm, she uses it as a fulcrum to swing her left foot up, above the pipe and through the spikes. With her left foot wedged between them, she is able to grab onto the spikes with both hands and pull herself high enough to see over the gate. She suddenly remembers the last lines of the verse:

I let him down with a silver chain,
And every link I called his name.

The empty streets and sidewalks out there, the darkened stores and warehouses and homes, the whole vast dark city itself, all seem to go on endlessly into the night. She is about to free herself from this cage. She is escaping into the city. Her right leg hangs in the air a few feet off the ground behind her. The dog doesn't growl or snarl. He doesn't even breathe loudly. He is silent and strikes like a snake. He clamps onto her leg with his powerful jaws and drags her backward, off the gate.

THE INVISIBLE PARROT

Guy walks into a bar with a parrot on his shoulder . . .

Actually Billy walks into a neighborhood grocery store, not a bar, and he's only pretending he has a parrot on his shoulder. He's trying to think of a new version of an old joke. When Billy's depressed or scared—and this morning he's both—he has imaginary conversations with himself.

The place is a combination grocery-liquor-cigar store smelling of three-day-old fish, sour milk and tobacco, on Alton Road a block north of Lincoln, between the hotels on the beach and the condos on the bay. Squeezed between a Burger King and a massage parlor, the store is dim and dingy—four narrow, crowded aisles with a single cash register operated by a thin Chinese woman in her fifties. Her arms are crossed and she's gazing at the ceiling deep in thought when Billy strolls in with his invisible parrot. He stops here several times a week on his way to or from work at the hotel and he sort of knows her, although they've never really talked.

She ignores him and he feels himself and the parrot fade. He figures she's compounding variable interest rates on randomly chosen sums and doesn't want to interrupt her calculations to say, *Hello, good morning, young man. What a pretty bird!* To which the parrot would say, *Thank you, ma'am. I'd like today's* Miami Herald *with the weekend real estate listings and a map of the city. My apartment has been condemned by the city and I need to find a clean, inexpensive place to live that accepts humans. Ha, ha.*

There are two other people in the store—a tall gray-faced black woman in her thirties and a slump-shouldered middle-aged Chinese man with a clipboard, probably the husband of the cashier, counting dented cans in aisle two and positioning the cans on the shelves to hide the dents. The black woman has voluminous hips stuffed into too-tight jeans and wears a dark green company uniform shirt with *Charlotte* sewn onto the right breast pocket. She looks like she's been up all night cleaning bathrooms at Mount Sinai Medical Center. He was up all night, too, packing his belongings to move out of his condemned apartment. He knows how she feels. Sort of. She feels hopeless. And invisible. But not to him: Billy sees her, and if he can see her—if one other person can know that's she's alive and in spite of everything still kicking—then she needn't feel hopeless, right? Same for him, if one other person can see him.

She picks up a liter of Diet Pepsi with one hand and a bag of potato chips with the other and lugs them to the register. Billy removes a newspaper from the rack and takes a city map from a second rack clipped to the wall. The black woman and Billy reach the register at the same time. She shoots Billy a sharp look: another pushy young white man. Not him. No way. He turns and checks out the candy stand.

She plunks the plastic jug and chips on the counter, sighs audibly and waits for the Chinese woman to acknowledge her presence. The black woman clears her throat, gets no response. She works a wrinkled envelope from her back pocket and studies a list written on it. Pressing the envelope flat on the counter she plucks a ball-point pen from a jar of pens next to the register, leans over the envelope and checks off the first two items on her list. Billy looks around her shoulder and reads the words written on the envelope in large hand-drawn capitals:

ATM

FOOD

PAY ELECTRIC

GET HAIR DONE

CALL ETHYLEEN

Something about the list tightens Billy's stomach into a fist. It's as if her whole life is written there. Charlotte will have already gone to the ATM and run her twenty-something-dollar bank balance down to zero. *Check.* Now she buys a liter of Diet Pepsi and a bag of potato chips for breakfast. *Check.* After Charlotte eats her breakfast sitting alone on a bench at the bus stop on Alton and Lincoln Road she'll walk to the Florida Power & Light office at the Stop & Shop on West, where she'll pay her overdue electric bill in cash because her checks have bounced too many times. *Check.* Charlotte will head for Jeannie's Cut-Right Cut-Rate Beauty Nook to get a wave put back in her hair. Seven bucks. *Check.* Now that she's feeling pretty Charlotte will buy a dollar phone card and call Ethyleen on her cell phone to tell her about it. *Check.* Then she'll take the bus back to Overton and walk to her building and step over toys and trash and broken glass up to her third-floor apartment. She has a teenage son who's supposed to be in school but is shooting hoops over at Franklin Park and an unemployed boyfriend who says he's looking for a job but has long since given that up and instead hangs in the 'hood getting high with his posse. She'll draw the shades in the cluttered bedroom, take off her clothes and put on a shortie nightgown. She'll set the alarm clock for 5:00 P.M. so she can make it back to the hospital in time. The night shift. Charlotte wraps her hair in a scarf, lies down in the unmade bed and immediately falls asleep. *Check.*

That's it, her life's checklist. Billy wonders what kind of list he'd make that would do the same for him.

☐ BUY NEWSPAPER AND CITY MAP

☐ FIND NEW PLACE TO LIVE

☐ GO TO WORK

☐ ASK TO GET PROMOTED FROM BUSBOY TO WAITER

☐ MOVE STUFF TO NEW PLACE AFTER WORK

Five items—the same number on his list as on Charlotte's. Suddenly he's angry at the Chinese woman for making Charlotte wait for no good reason. The woman seems to be deliberately ignoring him and his new friend.

"Hey, Missus! You got payin' customers here!"

The Chinese woman slowly turns and looks at him. She's chewing on a toothpick. For a few seconds she studies the items in his hands—the newspaper and map—and the two in Charlotte's—Diet Pepsi and bag of chips. She switches the toothpick from one side of her mouth to the other.

"Why you in such a big hurry?"

He's embarrassed now and wishes he'd let Charlotte make the complaint or just waited until the lady was ready to take their money. "I . . . I got to take a piss."

"No public restroom here."

The woman ambles to the register and rings up Charlotte's Diet Pepsi and chips and drops them into a plastic bag. Charlotte pays with four singles, grabs the change and without looking back walks quickly out to the street. Billy jiggles and hops up and down a couple of times as if he really does have to take a piss. The Chinese woman moves in slow motion, picks up his newspaper and map from the counter and runs them under the scanner.

When he opens his wallet all he has are two singles and a twenty. His last twenty till payday. The paper and the map together come to $6.45. He passes the twenty to the woman.

"This all you got? Too early to make change."

"Where can I get it changed?"

"Go to bank on the corner. They open at nine."

"That's like an hour and a half. I gotta get to work."

"Not my problem."

"I only got enough change for the paper."

"So buy paper."

Billy pays her with two quarters and makes for the door where he stops and turns back. "You know that woman in front of me?"

"She come in here all the time."

"So why did you make her wait like that? Seriously. That wasn't nice, lady."

"She on drugs. She all the time try to steal from us. Good-bye," the Chinese lady says and slams shut the cash drawer. She folds her arms across her chest again and goes back to her calculations.

Billy steps outside to the sunlit street. And there is Charlotte waiting for him. She looks plaintively into his eyes. He turns away and starts walking toward Lincoln.

"Can you help me out, mister? I got to get to my job in North Miami an' I need another dollar for the bus."

Billy stops and checks her out top to bottom. She's not the same person she was a minute ago. She's changed from being invisible to everyone but Billy into a junkie visible to all. Probably a clucker, a crackhead. "What about the money you just spent in there for junk food? That was enough for a bus to North Miami."

"I thought I had enough leftover, but I was wrong. I . . ."

"What about your list?"

"What list?"

"On the envelope. I seen it."

She pulls the same envelope from her back pocket and examines it. "You want it? I'll give it to you for a buck."

"I mean the things you wrote there."

"It was on the floor. Sometimes people lose envelopes with money in 'em. Even Chinese people."

"How come you checked things on the list? Like food and ATM."

She shrugs. "Why not?"

"Is your name Charlotte? Like it says on your shirt?"

"Maybe. Maybe not. You got any spare change, then?"

"No."

"Yeah, well, fuck you, then."

Slowly Billy pulls his wallet from his back pocket. He flips it open and removes the twenty-dollar bill and passes it to her.

She takes the bill without looking at it and stuffs it into her back pocket.

She hands him the envelope.

"No thanks," he says.

"It's yours now. You bought it, mister."

Billy waves his hands in front of his face.

The woman crumples the envelope in her fist and tosses it onto the sidewalk. "You have a nice day," she says and walks away.

For a full minute Billy stands and watches her. The parrot on his shoulder says, *Easy come easy go. Finders keepers losers weepers. What goes around comes around.*

Billy says to the parrot, "Just shut the fuck up."

THE OUTER BANKS

Ed pulled the RV off the road and parked it in a small paved lot, the front bumper kissing the concrete barrier, the large pale gray vehicle facing the sea, and Alice said, "Why are we stopping?"

The rain came in curtains off the Atlantic, one after the other, like the waves breaking against the sand, only slower, neither building nor diminishing. The couple watched the rain and the waves through the wide, flat windshield. There were no other vehicles in the lot and none in sight on the coastline road behind them. It was late fall, and the summer houses and rental cottages and motels were closed for the season.

"I don't know why. I mean, I do know. Because of the dog." He cracked open his window and relighted the cold stub of his cigar, and for a long while the couple sat in silence.

Finally she said, "So these are the famous Outer Banks of North Carolina."

"Yeah. Sorry about the weather," he said. " 'Graveyard of the Atlantic,' Alice."

"Yes. I know."

"Joke, Alice? Joke?"

She didn't answer him. A moment passed, and he said, "We've got to do something about the dog. You know that."

"What've you got in mind? Bury her in the sand? That's a real cute idea, Ed. Bury her in the sand and drive on our merry way, just like that." She looked at her hands for a moment. "I don't like thinking about it either, you know."

He eased himself from the driver's chair, stood uncertainly, and walked back through the living area and the tidy galley to the closet-sized bathroom, where he got down carefully on his knees and drew back the shower curtain and looked at the body of their dog. She was a black and white mixed breed, Lab and springer, lying on her side where Ed had found her this morning, when, naked, he'd gone to take a shower. He studied the dog's stiffened muzzle. "Poor bastard," he said.

"Maybe we should try to find a vet!" she called from the front.

"She's dead, Alice!" he hollered.

"They'll know how to take care of her, I meant."

Ed stood up. He was seventy-two; the simple things had

gotten very difficult very quickly—standing up, sitting down, getting out of bed, driving for longer than four or five hours. When they left home barely a year ago, none of those things had been difficult for him. That was why he had done it, left home, why they both had done it, because, while nothing simple was especially difficult for them, they were old enough to know that whatever they did not do or see now they would never do or see at all.

It was Alice's idea, too, not his alone—the romance of the open road, see America and die, master of your destiny, all that—although the actual plan had been his, to sell the house in Troy and all their furniture, buy and outfit the RV, map and follow the Interstate from upstate New York to Disney World to the Grand Canyon to Yosemite to the Black Hills, man, he'd always wanted to see the Black Hills of South Dakota, and Mount Rushmore was even grander and more inspirational than he'd hoped, then on to Graceland, and now the Outer Banks. He hadn't once missed the hardware store, and she hadn't missed the bank. They'd looked forward to retirement, and once there, had liked it, as if it were a vacation spot and they'd decided to stay year-round. There were no children or grandchildren or other close family—they were free as birds. "Snowbirds," they'd been called in Florida and out in Arizona. When they left home, their dog, Rosie, was already old, ten or eleven, he wasn't sure, they'd got her from the pound, but, Jesus, he hadn't figured on her dying like this. It was as if she had run out

of air, out of life, like a watch that had stopped because someone forgot to wind it.

He dropped his cigar butt into the toilet, looked at it for a
second and resisted flushing—she'd scowl when she saw it, he
knew, because it was ugly, even he thought so, but he shouldn't
waste the water—and walked heavily back to the front and sat
in the driver's chair.

"Vets are for sick animals. Not dead animals," he said
to her.

"I suppose you want to leave her in a Dumpster or just
drop her at the side of the road somewhere."

"We should've found a home for Rosie. When we left
Troy, I mean. Should've given her to some people or something, you know?" He looked at his wife, as if for a solution.
She was crying, though. Silently, with tears streaming down
her pale cheeks, she cried steadily, as if she had been crying for
a long time and had no idea how to stop.

He put a hand on her shoulder. "Alice. Hey, c'mon, don't
cry. Jesus, it's not the end of the world, Alice."

She stopped and fumbled in the glove compartment for a
tissue, found one and wiped her face. "I know. But what are we
going to do?"

"About what?"

"Oh, Ed. About Rosie. This," she said and waved a hand
at the rain and the sea. "Everything."

"It's my fault," he said. He stared at her profile, hoping she would turn to him and say no, it wasn't his fault, it wasn't anybody's. But she didn't turn to him; she said nothing.

Slowly, he rose from his seat again. He walked to the bathroom and pulled back the shower curtain. He kneeled down and gently lifted the dog in his arms, surprised that she was not heavier. Lying there she had seemed solid and heavy, as if carved of wood and painted, like an old, unused merry-go-round horse. He carried the dog to the side door of the RV and worked it open with his knee and stepped down to the pavement. The rain fell on him, and he was quickly drenched. He wore only a short-sleeved shirt and Bermuda shorts and sneakers, and all of a sudden he was cold. He carried the dog to the far corner of the parking lot, stepped over the barrier between the pavement and the beach, and walked with slow, careful steps through the wet sand toward the water. The rain blocked his vision and plastered white swatches of his hair to his skull and his thin clothes to his body.

Halfway between the parking lot and the water, he stopped and set the dog down. He was breathing rapidly from the effort. He wiped the rain from his eyes, got down on his hands and knees and started scooping sand. He pulled double handfuls of it away, worked down through the wet, gray sand to the dry sand beneath and kept digging, until finally he had carved a large hole. Still on his knees, he reached across the hole and drew the body of the dog into it. Her hair was wet and smelled the way it had when she was still alive. Then, slowly, carefully, he covered her.

When he was finished and there was a low mound where before there had been a hole, he turned around and looked back at the RV in the parking lot. He could see his wife staring out the windshield from the passenger's seat. He couldn't tell if she was looking at him or at the sea or what. He turned his gaze toward the sea. The rain was still coming steadily in curtains, one after the other.

He stood and brushed the crumbs of wet sand from his clothes, bare legs and hands and made his way back to the parking lot. When he had settled himself into the driver's chair, he said to his wife, "That's the end of it. I don't want to hear any more about it. Okay?" He turned the ignition key and started the motor. The windshield wipers swept back and forth like wands.

"Okay," she said.

He backed the RV around and headed toward the road. "You hungry?" he asked her.

She spoke slowly, as if to herself. "There's supposed to be a good seafood place a few miles south of here. It's toward Kitty Hawk. So that's good."

He put the RV into gear and pulled out of the lot onto the road south. "Fine," he said. "Too bad we have to see Kitty Hawk in the rain, though. I was looking forward to seeing it. I mean, the Wright brothers and all."

"I know you were," she said.

The cumbersome vehicle splashed along the straight, two-lane highway, and no cars passed. Everyone else seemed to be inside today, staying home.

Ed said, "We could keep going, y'know. Head for Cape Canaveral, check out the Space Center and all."

She said, "They shut the space program down, I thought."

"I guess maybe they did."

LOST AND FOUND

He knows her from some other crowded room, but can't remember which room or when. Good-looking brunette, broad forehead, high cheekbones—eastern European, he guesses. A little fleshy from drink and insufficient exercise. Fortyish, with minor evidence of wear: a younger woman's butch haircut laced with gray that she would color but doesn't believe she's old enough yet for a dye job, black pantsuit to hide her muffin top, red shoes. They're called pumps, he thinks.

He takes her in as she slips between strangers, not exactly on a beeline for his corner of the ballroom but not stopping to sniff the roses either. He likes to read people from a distance—that's what he calls it, reading people. Speed-reading. She's trying to disguise her intent, glancing at him as if by accident, then looking away as if she's not coming for him but for some guy on his right or left, one of these hearty fellows, hard drinks in hand, bellowing so as to impress each other and the occasional nearby woman with their intelligence and wit and the size of their annual bonus.

Like him, they're plumbing and heating supply sales managers, retailers and wholesalers from all over, most of them middle-aged and older men with wives at home. There are some wives here, of course, heavyset women in their fifties and sixties wearing pastel and silently monitoring their husbands' alcohol intake from their seats at the tables while keeping a wary eye on the few female sales reps working the room for new accounts. Maybe that's what she is, a manufacturer's sales rep he flirted with at some other January convention in some other Sunbelt city, and she enjoyed it enough to give him a second shot at writing her a purchase order. With female reps it's usually kitchen appliances and sinks or high-end bathroom fixtures. He'd definitely remember her if he'd signed on the first time around.

She half smiles and lets her left hand float toward his. Slight makeup overkill, large green eyes, mascara running from contacts worn only when she goes out. The nail polish matches the red pumps. No wedding ring, he notices. Recently divorced? She says, "Hello, Stanley."

He takes her hand in his, holds it a half second longer than he would a stranger's. "Well, hello! Nice to see you." He doesn't say "again." He's not 100 percent sure they're not strangers.

She knows his name, but why not, it's stuck to his jacket lapel. He flicks a glance across her breasts in search of a name tag, but there isn't one. Must not be a rep. Definitely not a hooker. Not friendly enough.

"You don't recognize me, do you, Stanley?"

"It would help if you wore your name on your chest like the rest of us." He flashes the smile he sometimes uses to change the subject.

"I work for the hotel. Remember? Events coordinator?"

"Right! Events coordinator." It was here in Miami, then, the Marriott. Had to have been five years ago, the last time the suppliers' National Business Association held their annual meeting here. Since then it's been Phoenix, New Orleans, Atlanta, Memphis. He met her in this very ballroom. Five years ago.

Her name is Ellen, that much rushes back, but not her last name. And not much else, though he feels his face heat up as if he's embarrassed. He's not sure if it's because he didn't recognize her right away or because of something that happened between them, something said or unsaid, done or undone, something he can't quite call to mind—like her last name—without her help. He's sure she remembers everything, her direct gaze tells him that much, and he is afraid that she expects him—or until this moment, expected him—to remember everything, too.

She looks mildly amused by his embarrassment. Forgiving.

He says her first name, "Ellen!" as if he's been waiting to say it since he got off the plane this afternoon. "You look terrific," he says and means it, up close she does look terrific, smart and energetic and good humored without being one of those scary, live-wired women who live on a permanent stage. She's a woman who keeps an interesting tension between high spirits and control. The sort of woman he's always been attracted to. Like his wife.

That's when he remembers. It was late the last night of the convention, and they ended up in his room, both a little drunk. How could he have forgotten? It wasn't the sort of thing that he's done more than once or twice in his entire twice-married life—in fact, now that he thinks of it, the first time he ended up in a hotel room alone with a woman who was not his wife was nearly twelve years ago. Not many months afterward, that woman became his second wife and eventually the mother of his three children. All the more reason he should have recognized Ellen right away, should even have anticipated seeing her here. And looked forward to meeting her again, or dreaded it. He's not sure which. He is sure he didn't sleep with her.

They met that first time at the registration table in the lobby. He said his last name, and without looking up she passed him an information packet and his plastic name tag. Then she glanced at him and quickly smiled, as if surprised by his good looks. He knew he was conventionally handsome. Not male model or movie star quality, just handsome for a plumbing and heating supplier.

"If you have any questions or need anything, don't hesitate to call me," she said. She reached into her purse, took out her business card and gave it to him. He held her card in both hands and read it, smiled back and thanked her by name. Damned attractive woman. Friendly too.

After that, they kept running into each other in the hotel, at first by accident in the lobby, then on the elevator, at the hotel gift shop where he'd gone for toothpaste and she was picking up a pack of cigarettes, and then in the evening deliberately at dinner in the main ballroom sitting next to each other as if they hadn't planned it, ducking the after-dinner speakers and heading for the hotel bar "for a nightcap" that lasted till midnight. They met for breakfast the next day and had lunch at a sidewalk café by the bay. They kept their voices low and their heads close.

With increasing speed they had dropped into personal, almost intimate conversations, and he thought of her as his only friend at the convention, although he was more than casually acquainted with dozens of the other managers here. He talked about his wife, Sharon, and his kids and described his life in Saratoga Springs, careful not to complain, but making his cloudy dissatisfaction with his life obvious. "It's a good town for raising kids. For owning a split-level house with a two-car garage, shopping at the malls, running a plumbing supply company."

She got it. "Sounds a little lonely," she said.

"Yeah, well, you can be lonely anywhere, I guess. Even in a crowd. Like here."

"Maybe especially in a crowd. Crowds can sting your heart when you're alone in the world. Like me."

He liked that phrase, "sting your heart." Not something Sharon would say. "C'mon, you're not really alone in the world. Attractive single woman, financially independent, exotic city like Miami, et cetera."

"Unmarried, no kids, no close family nearby, et cetera. No steady boyfriend. Just a cat named Spooky to greet me when I come home from work. That's being alone in the world, Stanley."

"And you're not lonely?"

She shrugged. "No more than you, I suspect. With your wife and kids and minivan."

"Maybe not."

She had quickly become the only person at the convention he wanted to talk and drink with and sneak out onto the terrace to escape the crowd and smoke cigarettes with—the same brand, he remembers, American Spirits, which she jokingly claimed were good for you because the tobacco is organic. They were both trying to quit. Without stating it, they felt smarter and sexier, especially when together, than the people surrounding them. Whenever they spoke of the conventioneers and their wives, they spoke with irony and slight, but not unkind, condescension. Neither of them took the convention or the plumbing and heating supply industry seriously.

To him, regardless of which room they happened to find themselves in, Ellen was definitely the most desirable woman in it. And looking around at his colleagues, most of whom were overweight, badly dressed, red faced and loud, he figured he was the most desirable man in the room. At least to her. The competition wasn't exactly stiff, however.

He knew by then that Ellen was thirty-four, fifteen years younger than he was, divorced, and her parents lived in Charlotte, North Carolina, where she'd been raised. She'd come to Miami to study marketing at Florida International University. The week after graduation she'd eloped with a man a decade older who had been her statistics professor. "We lasted four years. Luckily there were no kids. Turned out the professor still had a thing about sleeping with his students," she told him. "Male as well as female," she added.

"Weird."

"What, sleeping with students, or swinging both ways?"

"Swinging both ways, I guess."

"Not so weird. You'd be surprised how many handsome male college professors swing both ways. It's not about sex. They're scared of sex. They want acolytes. But maybe it's Miami," she added and laughed.

"Miami is a pretty sexy city."

"That's marketing directed at northerners, Stanley. Don't

fall for it. Miami's no sexier than Saratoga Springs, New York."

His turn to laugh. "Yeah, right."

The last night of the convention they slipped away from the closing party, crossed the lobby and stepped outside and lighted cigarettes. He remembers the moist smell of the Gulf Stream in the warm offshore breeze. A pair of palm trees clattered in the wind. The driver at the head of a line of waiting cabs flicked his high beams at them.

"You want to go somewhere?" Stanley said.

"No."

He waved the driver off. "Where's your place?"

"The Gables. Coral Gables. It's a ways."

"Want to go up to my room and raid the minibar for a nightcap?"

She looked away and then down at her feet, turned and rubbed out her cigarette in the standing ashtray next to the door and said, "Sure."

When they turned to reenter the hotel, five of his colleagues, all men, came jostling out the revolving glass door. Stanley guided Ellen around them by the elbow. He knew one of the men slightly, a beefy guy in his fifties named Bernie who ran a supply house in Syracuse.

"Hey, Stan, c'mon out with us!" Bernie said. "We're going over to the beach and do a little sightseeing. South Beach, man! The night's still young!"

"Thanks but no thanks, Bernie. I've got an early flight

out tomorrow." He gave the revolving door a push and Ellen walked through and he followed.

Bernie laughed and said, "Yeah, sure."

His room was on the twenty-seventh floor with a wide, floor-to-ceiling view of Biscayne Bay and the port where the cruise ships, parked like pale dirigibles, waited for their passengers to arrive from the north, and beyond the bay the glittering lights and pulsing neon of South Beach. East of the condo towers, hotels and clubs of South Beach, beneath the scraps of cloud lit pink from below, he could see the Atlantic Ocean, a long dark arm speckled with moonlight.

He opened the minibar and took out an unopened half bottle of California chardonnay, unscrewed the metal cap and poured the wine into two glasses. He counted how many drinks he'd already had tonight. Two scotches at the reception and at the final dinner four glasses of wine. He didn't feel drunk but knew he probably was.

"Nice view to wake up to," she said. She sat on the bed and, pinning her gaze to the view, reached down, unstrapped her shoes without looking and flipped them off her feet. He walked to her and placed her wineglass on the bedside table and went back to the window, turned toward the sea and watched her reflection in the glass. She wore a simple black sleeveless dress, he remembers, and a necklace of rough, heavy, semiprecious stones on a leather cord. She had beautiful slender legs. She removed her hooped earrings and laid them on the bedside table next to the wineglass. She took a sip of the wine.

"Are you going to just stand there?"

"I don't know."

She was silent for a moment. Then said, "You don't know."

She reached down and slipped her shoes back on and buckled the thin straps. He had asked for this, had engineered it, with her help, of course, but he could have blocked it anywhere along the line, just flirted over a weekend, basked in the glow of attention from an attractive younger woman, maybe even indulged in a sexual fantasy or two, all harmless, and caught his early Sunday flight home with a clear conscience, no complications, no secret entanglements. But instead he'd let each step lead to the next on a meandering path that he knew all along would end at this moment. She hooked her earrings on and stood up.

Was he really as lonely as he'd let her believe? If not actually suffering from his marriage, was he bored by it, feeling invisible in it, like an old piece of furniture that can't be moved or replaced without moving or replacing everything else in the room, so you just leave it where it is and ignore it? It wasn't his age, he assures himself, the so-called midlife crisis men go through in their late forties and early fifties. He was young for his age. Especially then, five years ago. He had no desire to trade his minivan for a red Porsche, join a health club, abandon his striped Hanes boxers for black Calvin Klein low-rise briefs. And it wasn't just any attractive younger woman he'd been courting—but not actively seducing—all weekend, as if to prove a point about his desirability to himself and the other guys like Bernie. It wasn't male vanity. It was Ellen herself, a very specific woman whose smoky low voice, green eyes, dry humor and bright, interesting words, and yes, her slender legs, that had got to him. That, and the way she made him feel about himself.

She was angry, he remembers now. Which is probably why he wanted to forget that night, why he actually succeeded in forgetting it and the way Ellen had made him feel, until here she was again, five years older, yet still that very particular woman who made him visible to himself, funny, smart, good looking, and lonely. These were feelings about himself that he had lost bit by bit over the years of his marriage and middle age, small increments of loss, so that he wasn't even aware of the loss, until that night when they ended up alone in his room at the Marriott. Lost and, because of her, found. And then all of a sudden lost again. Until now.

"It's okay, Stanley, you don't have to pretend. I know you didn't recognize me at first. And maybe still don't. I know you don't remember."

"The truth is, I didn't want to remember. Me, I mean. Not you."

"Why? You didn't do anything wrong. You almost did. But you didn't."

"Maybe that's why. I didn't want to remember what I lost that night. And what I found. I wanted to forget that too."

She gave a hard little laugh and stepped back. "I wish I believed it. What do you think you found and wanted to forget, Stanley? Not true love, that's for sure."

"No. Something else." He's about to tell her to forget it, whatever it was, it can't be described. Not by him, anyhow. But instead he hears himself say, "My heart got stung. I could feel it beating, and for the first time in years, maybe in my whole life, I knew I was alive."

"And it scared you."

"It's like, if you know you're alive, you know you're going to die."

"So you decided to forget that you were alive."

"Yes."

"Which is like dying before your time."

"Yes. It is."

He remembers her standing beside the bed, half turned toward the door, ready to leave his room. He walked across to her and put his arms around her and kissed her gently on the lips. She kept her mouth closed, her lips tight, and after a few seconds shook free of his embrace.

He said, "I'm sorry."

She said, "Don't be. You didn't do anything."

He said, "That's why I'm sorry."

"Goodbye, Stanley."

He turned back to the darkened window and watched her reflection cross the room to the door, open it, and leave. The door closed slowly behind her.

She says, "Well, it's been good to see you again. You haven't changed, Stanley."

He says, "Yes, I have."

She says, "Goodbye, Stanley," and makes her way back through the crowded ballroom toward the exit.

SEARCHING FOR VERONICA

This is what she told me. It came almost from nowhere. I happened to be sitting next to her at the bar in Gustav's, a German-style pub and grill in the Portland International Airport between Gates 7 and 9 on Concourse C. I was waiting out the night for a storm-delayed Minneapolis flight. I think she was already there when I came in, but maybe not. I remember the bar was otherwise empty. The local TV news and weather was on without the sound.

We hadn't even exchanged names when she started her story. I might have smiled and said hello or something bland to jumpstart a conversation and show her I wasn't going to hit on her, the way you do if you're a male traveler and you start talking to a woman in a bar. She was a worn-down fifty, a basically good-looking woman with a friendly smile and a lot of mileage who I figured was a waitress whose shift at one of the airport restaurants had just ended. Not a traveler. Turned out I was right and it was Wendy's. Anyhow, this is what she told me.

As if we're old friends she said, "Whenever the TV news runs a story about finding the body of some unidentified woman in the bushes by the river I wonder if the woman is my friend Veronica. And if I'm downtown I glance into alleys as I pass, hoping to see her alive. You probably think that's weird."

I said no. But I did think it was weird. Not the content of what she told me, but the fact that she was telling it to a stranger. That and the way she told it.

She said to me, "Sometimes the next day I even take the bus to the city morgue and try to identify the body, since I can still picture Veronica's tattoos and piercings all these years later."

I asked her who was Veronica.

She said, "It was the summer I turned thirty, a couple months after Carl walked out on us. Helene was seven going on eight."

I said, "Helene is your daughter, then?"

She said, "Yeah. I was struggling just to survive and take care of her, so I swallowed hard and gave the back bedroom in our apartment, the room we'd been using for the cats, to this girl, to Veronica. She'd stayed over after my birthday party and was trying to cut loose of her idiot biker boyfriend and get off of drugs. The cats and their litter box we moved to the screened porch overlooking the back alley."

She said, "I think Veronica and her boyfriend were into meth pretty heavy. Not just using, manufacturing in some trailer outside town, and selling, at least her boyfriend was. Rudy was his name, I can recall that even today, what, almost twenty years later, because when she talked that was what she talked about, Rudy Rudy Rudy. She drove me nuts with her fixation on this guy, who to me was just some piece-of-shit biker who liked to get high and boost his manhood by whacking his girlfriend on the head every few days to make her cry and say, 'Stop, stop, please, Rudy, stop!' You know the type."

I knew the type, I told her, but the woman kept talking as if I hadn't said anything. It was not exactly like she was alone, but more like I wasn't a real person sitting next to her at Gustav's bar. It was as if she was telling her story to a camera on a reality TV show and had already told a version of it many times. I didn't care, I was just killing time and trying not to let my flight delay get me down, and she had a friendly face and a nice whiskey-and-cigarette voice.

She said to me, "I had an okay job at a travel agency then. Portland was into connecting with the Orient and all these fast-tracked techno-yuppies were booking weekends in Tokyo and Hong Kong and writing it off their taxes, so even though I'd been slam-dumped by Carl, who'd ridden off into the Hawaiian sunset with his dental hygienist, I was doing fine, no food stamps, no handouts necessary, except I had to work nine to five six days a week and needed somebody to take care of Helene after she got home from school. Which is where Veronica comes in."

I didn't say anything and looked off at the TV, checking the weather. The midwestern storms were moving east. She took a sip of her drink and plunged ahead. Her timing was pretty good, I noticed.

She said, "Veronica was a tall girl, taller than me anyhow, with a bunch of piercings on her face and elsewhere that I could guess but didn't want to know about and homemade tats pretty much everywhere you looked and so skinny you could see her spine through her T-shirt like she had an eating disorder, anorexia or bulimia, one of those, only it was probably from the meth and whatever other chemicals she was putting into her body then, because later I found out she definitely had a healthy appetite. I wasn't that much older than Veronica—she was nineteen or early twenties, I think, so okay, a decade—but right away I felt motherly toward her. Maybe because of Helene, who I was afraid would turn out like Veronica if she didn't have me as a mother.

"She showed up following the shadow of Rudy, who came to the party with the three biker brothers from downstairs who came because you couldn't throw even a small party in that building without those guys sniffing at the door, six-pack in hand. None of my female friends, especially the single ones, objected because the brothers were young and very good looking and lifted weights and you could hook up with one of them if you wanted. We did that sort of thing back then. We were still young. We called them Huey, Dewey and Louie. I can't remember their real names now. They had jobs and were basically harmless although not too bright and were always holding good weed. But they sometimes brought along a wacko friend or two like Rudy who were into chemicals or crack or both and on the edge of freaking which made everybody nervous. The next day one of the brothers would come upstairs and apologize, which I didn't mind at all, especially after Carl left.

"Anyhow, Veronica wasn't in danger of freaking. She was just sad looking with big dark circles under her eyes like she hadn't slept in a week, chopped-off dyed black hair that needed a good shampoo, little flat-chested nipples poking the front of her dirty T-shirt and jeans all torn on purpose below the crotch and at the knees like it's a fashion statement."

I downed the last of my drink and ordered refills for both of us. "It's a good story you're telling," I said to the woman, and we clinked glasses.

She said, "Yeah, well, Veronica's dead now. Or at least I'm pretty sure she's dead. But maybe not. It was twenty years ago. Back then I figured if somebody doesn't take care of her fast she isn't going to last the summer. I mean, she thought Rudy was taking care of her. It was the early nineties, remember. All over the country teenage kids were checking out or being kicked out and nobody knew how to stop it. People weren't experimenting with drugs like in the sixties anymore, they were dosing themselves with drugs. It wasn't about fun anymore. Those kids, the ones who survived the nineties, they're parents themselves now with kids of their own, some with grandkids, so what does that tell us? All they know about reality is what their parents found time to teach them. And what did we know?"

"Not much," I said.

"Not much that was good. That was when county sheriffs and federal prosecutors were busting day-care centers and kindergartens for child sex abuse and weird satanic rituals and making kiddie porn. Remember?"

I told her I thought that was in the eighties.

She said, "It was in the nineties, too. You didn't know what to believe. People were confused. I was glad Helene was still a little girl, even though it kind of fucked up my downtime, if you know what I mean. Because she was so dependent and all."

I said I knew what she meant. "I helped raise four kids of my own," I told her. "All adults now."

She said to me, "Anyhow, Rudy flipped out at my birthday party and started throwing my set of good wedding present steak knives one by one at the door that led from the kitchen into the living room, and when I bitched at him he puts down the remaining three or four steak knives and pulls out this big sheath knife he's wearing on his belt and throws it so hard it penetrates six inches right through the door. Everybody goes silent. Helene hides behind my skirt and starts to cry.

"Fortunately, Huey, Dewey and Louie muscled Rudy and his bowie knife out of the apartment, leaving Veronica nodding out on the couch, missing the whole show, although it was probably one she'd seen many times before. Afterward, scared that Rudy might come back alone, everyone split. So now it's just me, Helene and Veronica alone in the apartment. Happy fucking birthday. We never even got to the cake part.

"I double-locked the door, threw a blanket over Veronica, put Helene to bed and went to bed myself, but Helene was still scared and wanted to sleep in my bed with me, so I let her. Rudy didn't come back to get Veronica for three days, like he'd forgotten where he left her. But by then I'd gotten into her head a little, or maybe she arrived that night already primed to dump Rudy and kick drugs and only needed a little reinforcement from a third party, so to speak, like from a role model, an older independent woman able to take care of herself and her seven-year-old child."

"Like you," I said. "You and Helene."

"Yeah, like me. Me and Helene. The back bedroom already had a mattress on the floor and I put Carl's old sleeping bag and a lamp back there and hung a sheet over the window for privacy. I gave her some of my old T-shirts and jeans which were way short in the legs but she said she liked the pedal pusher look. Once she got rested she was real polite. Just not talkative.

"Veronica didn't appear to own anything and didn't have any money. She was like a child in certain ways. I had to buy her a toothbrush and let her borrow my shampoo and personal hygiene items and told her to eat whatever she wanted from the fridge and cupboards, which I sort of regretted once she got going because she was like a dog that's lived on the streets all her life and thinks she's never going to get another decent meal. By Sunday, not two days in, I had to restock practically everything, even the little boxed juices and Cheetos I kept for Helene's TV snacks.

"At breakfast the Monday after the party, we had our little talk. I asked Veronica if she'd walk Helene to school because I was supposed to get to the agency early to start learning a new computer program for booking airfares. Computers were just entering the travel industry then and everybody was scared of them, especially me because in school I was always lousy at math. Mainly I have people skills.

"Veronica goes, 'Sure, whatever,' which was sort of her default answer to any question put to her, but she said it so nicely and with a smile that you didn't mind.

"I told her, 'Here's the deal. You need a place to get your shit together. And I need a babysitter.' My old babysitter had just quit to work for this recently divorced female professor at Reed College who'd offered her twice what I could pay. I had permission to bring Helene to the office on Saturdays, so if Veronica could walk Helene home from school every weekday and stay with her till I got out of work, she could keep the back room. Plus I'd pay her five bucks an hour for babysitting twenty hours a week, which came to a hundred bucks a week. It was a stretch, but I had a little saved and a raise coming once I learned the new computer program.

" 'But no Rudy,' I told her. 'And no drugs. Except maybe if you want to burn a little weed with me in the evenings. That's up to you.' I knew I shouldn't be smoking in the apartment with her trying to quit using, but I needed my weed. In those days after Carl left I didn't want to give up my few remaining pleasures, and weed was definitely one. Still is.

"She seemed excited and said, 'No problem!' Helene was happy with the deal too. Veronica was like her new best friend and playmate. All weekend when Veronica wasn't asleep in her room she was stretched out beside Helene on the living room floor watching Helene's favorite TV shows with her, even the cartoons, and talking about them with her like she and Helene were kids the same age. Maybe that's another reason why I keep looking for her all these years later."

"Could be," I said. "Makes sense."

She went on with her story as if I hadn't said anything. "With me, though, she talked almost not at all, even when I asked about Rudy, if she had been living with him for long and so forth. Instead of words she answered with a humming sound, which I took to be a yes. When I asked where she was from originally she said, 'Here,' which I took to mean Portland. When I asked if her parents were still alive she nodded yes and said her mother was alive but she wasn't sure about her father and crinkled her brow like it was painful to think about them, so I decided not to push it. I figured she was another of those throwaway kids who cross their mother or father or stepfather somehow and get tossed out or walk out and live on their own from about the age of thirteen or fourteen. Who knew what she'd done to survive? All she had to trade on was her body and her youth, and with the piercings and tattoos, not to mention the drugs, she'd done a lot to destroy her body, and the passage of time was doing the same to her youth, the way it does to everyone's. Pretty soon she wouldn't have anything to trade on, except loyalty to assholes like Rudy."

I told the woman that I could dig it, as I had someone like that in my own family. I didn't say whether it was someone like the parents who tossed their child out or like the daughter who walked out on them, but in fact it was both.

She said, "So okay, then you can imagine how I felt when I got home from work that evening and the first thing Helene tells me is that the man who threw the knife at the door was here. 'But he's gone now,' she says. 'Veronica told him to fuck off.'

"I said that's great but she shouldn't say fuck. The kitchen was all neat and clean, spotless actually, much cleaner than when I do it, dishes washed and everything put away. I went into the living room and it was the same there. She'd even folded my laundry and stacked it neatly on my bed. She was in Helene's room putting away Helene's dozen Barbies and all their flimsy wardrobes and accessories.

"I said, 'So you told Rudy to fuck off?'

"She just smiled.

"I said, 'Good girl,' and thought that was the end of ol' Rudy. But of course it wasn't. Any more than her being clean for a few weeks was the end of her using drugs. But for a while, for a week or ten days, though she talked about Rudy constantly, she referenced him strictly in the negative, saying things out of the blue like, 'I can't believe I stayed with such an asshole,' or when I offered to let her use my phone in case she wanted to call somebody to say where she was, she goes, 'Rudy never let me call anybody.' I guess there wasn't anyone she wanted to call, though, because she never used the phone that I know of, and people didn't have cell phones then.

"It must've been obvious to her by now that I wasn't going to rip her off or drop a dime on her with her mother or some social worker and certainly not the cops, so she was talking to me more easily. Plus she was making eye contact with me and not just with Helene, which she wouldn't do at first, like an animal that's been abused by adult humans in the recent past and only expects more of the same. By this time I was really into mothering her. Something about her childlike physical awkwardness and her ignorance of the world, which usually make

me impatient with people, in her case made me feel protective.
Also I liked her company. Nights were a lot less lonesome in
the apartment than they had been. I'd gotten over her pierced
eyebrows, nostrils, ears and lips and had even started liking
her tattoos, especially the Rastafarian lion's head on her right
shoulder. The rattlesnake around her left wrist and the World
Trade Center in New York on her upper back were cool, too.
This was before nine-eleven, of course. Someone other than
Veronica must've tattooed the Trade Center because it was on
her back, but even so, I could tell from the others, since she'd
drawn them herself and tattooed the ones she could reach, that
Veronica had a real talent for art.

"All the time, though, like it's her only subject, Veronica
is talking about Rudy, only I notice it's not as negative as before. Slowly certain positives are creeping in, like, 'Rudy's this
amazing mechanic that can fix any kind of bike and even fixes
cars for his friends who have them,' and one night we're burning a pretty inferior joint, regular ditch weed, and she says,
'Y'know, Rudy grows the best boom in Oregon, but he'd never
show me his patch. He said it was to protect me in case I ever
got busted.'

"'Yeah, right,' I say. 'Mister Fucking Protective.' Obviously she needed a lot more instruction and self-confidence in
order to kick this guy. Still, although on a deep level I know
better, I'm telling myself this is turning into a successful home-
detox-slash-rehab, and I'm thinking of tossing another party to

finish celebrating my thirtieth. Plus I want to introduce Veronica to some new people so she won't be so dependent on me and Helene for company, when one Friday I come home from work and the second I walk through the door I know Rudy's been in the apartment."

I asked her how she could tell.

She said, "I could smell him. Grease, oil, gasoline fumes and something coldly chemical, almost medicinal. My first thought of course is where is Helene? That junkie punk bitch Veronica better not put my baby in danger or I'll kill her, I'm thinking as I go from room to room, until I find Helene in her bedroom down on the floor marrying Barbie and Ken with Share a Smile Becky as the bridesmaid. Everything looks okay, even the cats are there for the wedding, so I give her a hug and say, 'Where's Veronica?'

"Helene says, 'They went out, her and the man who threw the knife.'

"I asked her a few more questions, like how long was he in the apartment and how long ago did they go out, which turned out to be only a few minutes of each, and Veronica promised she'd be right back, which in fact she was, while I was still sitting there on the floor with Helene. She comes into the bedroom and leans against the doorframe and says, 'Awesome you're home. I was just getting rid of Rudy. On account of how you feel about him and all.'"

I said to the woman, "That's really good, right? That

Veronica was just getting rid of Rudy?" I was into her story by now and was starting to hope everything would turn out for the best, even though I knew from the way she'd begun her story that it wouldn't.

She said, "Yeah, right, really good. Not. Because when Veronica shoots me this big intense smile, I can tell right away from how she's handling her body and her breathing rate and her lying smile that she's high, and it isn't from weed, it's crack or meth. Which means that anything she says is pure bullshit. She says she has to pee and goes into the bathroom and closes the door. And of course that's bullshit too. It's just to keep me from looking at her.

"Since the girl doesn't know what's real or isn't real, there's no way I'm going to know it either. That's the way it goes down with junkies. They live in their own private story, even when they're not high. They make up and shape reality with their jones, and if you buy even a small part of it, your own reality gets infected by it, until their jones is yours too, and all the time twenty-four-seven you're thinking about whether she's high or not, holding or not, going to rip you off to buy drugs or not, telling the truth or not, or if she even *knows* the truth. It's like a virus. Their sickness becomes your sickness. The only safe response is to quarantine yourself off from them, don't listen to word one of their elaborate explanations for their actions or inactions. Assume everything is a lie and just throw them out of the house. Even if it's your own kid. Which is what I did."

"You mean Helene?" I ask her.

"No, Veronica! It's like you can't think about the consequences. You can't think about what'll happen to her now down there on the streets traipsing after the Rudys of the world until finally he decides she's too high-maintenance and is losing her looks, so he tosses her out like garbage for somebody even worse to scoop up, because no matter how far down the ladder of men she goes there's always some dump picker on the rung below glad to grab what little body and soul she's got left. That's why I believe Veronica is dead. She could've hooked up with one of the hundreds of losers heading south to Cali these days, of course, and maybe she did, or she could've gotten busted for manufacture and distribution and has been doing time at Coffee Creek Correctional down in Wilsonville. But something tells me she never left Portland. Maybe because in spite of the lousy climate I stayed here myself even after the dot-com bubble burst back in 2001 and I lost my job at the agency and had to go on welfare until I got hired at Wendy's. Because this is where Helene grew up. If she'd been busted and sent to Coffee Creek I would have heard about it from Huey, Dewey or Louie, although since they moved back to Eugene to start their own motorcycle repair shop I never see them anymore. But somebody would have told me. Everyone knew how attached

I was to that girl and how rotten I felt when I had to throw her out on the street."

I said, "You don't mean Helene, do you? You sure we're still talking about Veronica?"

"Yes, of course," she said. "I've never once run into her anywhere in the city, and Portland isn't that big and there are only a few neighborhoods where people like her, or like me for that matter, can afford to live. Like I said, I look for her everywhere, and you'd think I'd see her standing in line outside one of the soup kitchens or panhandling downtown or waiting in the rain for one of the homeless shelters to open. But I haven't. That's why I think she's dead.

"Anyhow, when Veronica finally came out of the bathroom that day I was waiting for her in the living room by the door with a trash bag filled with the few things she'd accumulated while living with me, the T-shirts and flip-flops and some underwear I'd laid on her and the junk she'd bought with the hundred bucks a week I was paying her, like a half-dozen CDs and a stack of fashion magazines that she liked to cut up and turn into these weird Goth-type collages and a pair of sunglasses that she wore just for looks, since the sun never shines in Portland.

" 'Here's all your shit. Take it and get out,' I told her. 'We're done, you and me.'

"She stared at me, wide-eyed and openmouthed like she was in shock. Her teeth were already starting to rot from the meth, and for a second I could see how she was going to look a few years from now, and I wanted to cry for her. I wanted to change my mind and hug her and believe whatever bullshit explanation she offered for having let that scumbag criminal into the apartment and then going off with him to get high while my daughter was still a vulnerable little girl, at least in my mind she was. But I couldn't. I had to be strong. I told her I don't want to have to change the locks to the apartment, so give me the keys.

"She doesn't say anything. Just hands over the keys.

"'Now go,' I tell her.

"'Where can I go?' she says in her little girl's voice.

"'Anywhere. Just not here.'

"'I was only trying to get rid of him without getting him pissed at me,' she says. 'He gets real mean when he's pissed.'

"'Don't talk. Just go,' I told her. I pulled open the door for the girl and she stepped out to the hall and turned back one last time.

"'I bet someday you'll be sorry you did this to me,' she said.

"'Only if you turn up dead,' I told her. It was the first time I thought it. But I had to take the chance on her turning up dead. It was like she hadn't given me any other choice. As a mother, I mean. I was only trying to save my daughter from ending up like Veronica, that's all. That was so long ago. But it's why every time I read in the paper or hear on the evening news that some young woman's unidentified body has been found down along the Willamette River or in Washington Park or in a vacant lot in Northeast Portland, I take the bus over to the morgue on Northwest Nicolai Street near the port, and I offer to identify the body, since I know all her tattoos and most of her piercings. But so far it hasn't been her. It's been some other young woman. The guys at the morgue, they know me now and know why I'm there. I don't even have to tell them that I'm searching for Veronica. Of course, they probably think I killed somebody and am checking to see if the body's been discovered yet."

I ordered another round of drinks for both of us, our third. I said to her, "When you go down to the morgue, you're not searching for Veronica. You're searching for Helene, aren't you? All along you've been talking about your daughter, Helene. She'd be twenty-six or twenty-seven now, right? Helene, I mean. You kicked Helene out of your apartment. Veronica, if she's alive, would be in her early forties. If she existed in the first place."

She said, "You don't understand! I'm looking for them both. I might be the only one who can identify them, you know. It's like I'm having a bad dream, and I want to wake up from it, but I'm afraid that when I do, the reality will be worse than the dream. I don't even know your name," she said, almost as an afterthought.

I told her my first name and asked for hers.

She said, "Russell is a nice name. You don't hear it much

anymore, though. I'm Dorothy. You don't hear that one much anymore, either."

We both went silent then and for a few minutes watched the end of a Trail Blazers game on the TV above the bar. Without looking down from the screen she said, "You're right. About Helene, I mean, and me having to kick her out and it being recent. A year and a half ago is recent, right? But you're wrong about Veronica. She existed. It all happened the way I said, and I've been searching for her ever since. Sometimes I thought I found her in Helene, especially after Helene got busted two years ago for dealing meth for her piece-of-shit boyfriend and spent six months at Coffee Creek and had to move back in with me when she got out." She sighed loudly, longingly, like a smoker wanting to step outside for a cigarette, and said, "Sometimes it feels like I've spent my whole adult life searching for Veronica." Then she suddenly grabbed my sleeve and laughed, the first time she'd laughed all night. It was a slightly mocking laugh at something she found ridiculous. She said, "Maybe *I'm* Veronica! You ever think of that, Russell?"

I turned and looked at her face and tried to look into and beyond her eyes, but her eyes coldly kicked my gaze back out. She was smiling, almost in triumph.

I said, "No! Not until this moment. But now I do. Now I think in this story, your story, you *are* Veronica. And you're Helene, the daughter, too. And you're Dorothy, the mother. And I think all three of you combined and did something very bad together. I think that's the reason whenever they discover the body of an unidentified young woman you go down to the morgue."

I stood up and waved for the check and paid for our drinks. "You're not looking for Veronica or Helene," I said. "You're looking for someone else, someone the three of you did a very bad thing to. Someone whose name you haven't revealed yet. And that's what you've been trying to tell me tonight. And trying not to tell me."

"I'm only telling you what I know, Russell."

"That's why you scare me. It's like you said about Veronica and junkies like her. They live in their own private story, even when they're not high. You said it's like a virus. Their sickness becomes your sickness. You said the only safe response is to quarantine yourself off from them. You said to assume everything is a lie. And that's exactly what I'm doing now. Good night," I said, "whoever you are. Wherever you are. Whatever you've done." I left the bar then and, shaken, walked straight to the gate to wait for my flight to Minneapolis.

THE GREEN DOOR

The Piano Hollywood is a piano bar squeezed between the casino and the hotel at the Seminole Hard Rock Hotel & Casino Hollywood, and like I deal cards instead of drinks the guy wants me to tell him the rules for Texas Hold'em. I know the rules, of course—who doesn't?

This guy doesn't. He's a somewhat oversized, maybe fifty-year-old pear-shaped dude with pink skin and a thinning gray-blond comb-over. He's wearing a blue-on-gold striped bow tie and a tan tropical-weight suit that at first I think is J. C. Penney or Sears, only when I have a chance to check the lines and workmanship close up I decide it's quality garb, nice cloth, probably Italian with a two-K setback, and the problem is not the suit, it's the guy's Sears, Roebuck body.

He's on his second Long Island iced tea when he pops the

Texas Hold'em question. It's early, a little after four in the afternoon, and the Piano is quiet—the day-trippers from the Fort Lauderdale and Miami old-age homes are over at the slots giving away their social security checks and the high rollers like bats in their caves are just waking up—so I give him the short form. I tell him about hole cards, the burn card, which amateurs sometimes think is the dealer cheating, but it's the opposite. I describe the preflop and the flop and the turn and the river, by which time the guy's eyes are glazed. He's going to get skinned eight different ways, I think. I tell him he should watch a few games before putting any chips on the table. But then I lie and say it's like seven-card stud, only simpler. For some reason a part of me doesn't feel like protecting the guy from himself.

He thanks me a little too much and orders another Long Island iced tea. I've got my back to him, jiggering the contents into an ice-filled glass—vodka, tequila, rum, gin, triple sec, sweet-and-sour mix and a splash of Coke. It's an alcohol mashup for drinkers who don't like the taste of alcohol but want to get wasted. While I'm pouring the mix into the shaker, out of nowhere he asks me in a too-loud voice, "Where can a fellow find himself some interesting sexual companionship for a few hours?" He's southern, Georgia or South Carolina, with a suburban, gated-community accent. You see a lot of them down here, men and women both, mostly good Christians sniffing for stuff they can't get back home.

I whack the shaker once and fill the glass from it, making sure there's a signature touch of fizz at the top, and plant a lemon wedge on the edge and set it in front of him. "Depends," I say.

"On what, pray tell." He takes a sip of his drink, closes his eyes and smiles appreciatively, like he's a connoisseur of Long Island iced teas and this one's a ten.

"Depends on how much you want to spend. And whether you have a car and are willing to drive down to South Beach or over to Fort Lauderdale or need to stay here on the rez. You bedding down at the Hard Rock?" I ask him.

He says yes, he's at the Hard Rock on business, but he has a rental car and can drive to wherever the women are. He calls them "ladies of the night." I can't tell if he's being funny or is just a total cracker asshole. I'm in my sixties, and it's the first time I've heard the expression.

"Also it depends on what sort of action you're looking for," I say.

He sips his drink with his eyes closed again. "I wouldn't mind a variety of activities. Something a little *de trop,* if you know what I mean."

I don't speak French but I get his drift. I explain that if he wants something other than the two or three more popular items on the menu he'll probably have to leave the rez, because the Seminoles run a pretty tight ship. "They're first and foremost in the gaming industry, you understand. They don't mind a working girl or two trolling the casino or the strip malls, so long as the girls are discreet and do their transacting in private, but the Seminoles are businesspeople and need to look squeaky clean. Even if they're not, exactly." I can add that because, although I'm told I look like a Seminole, I'm Jewish and am paid by the Piano, which is independently owned by Brits from Hong Kong.

"That's why I'm here!" he says. "To do business with the Seminoles! I'm hoping to open a chapel and meditation center at the resort. My partners and I are franchising prayer and meditation centers at Indian casinos all across the country. We've got over sixty up and running and another twenty-seven under contract."

"Sort of like fast food franchises?"

"In a sense, yes. The Indians really get it. They're a very spiritual people, you know, the Indians. The true genius of America, however, is marketing," he goes on. "We use Starbucks as a template. And the Hard Rock Cafe itself. The only difference is that our product is not coffee or food and alcohol or musical acts, and it's certainly not gambling. Our product is nondenominational spiritual space."

"A product that's invisible. Very cool. Any complaints, you can blame the customer. Better than selling bottled tap water," I say, kidding him a little. Although I'm an observant Jew in some ways, I'm very secular in others and don't believe in anything that's invisible, except atoms and molecules, and even about them I'm agnostic.

"Let's go back to our previous conversation," he says. "Concerning the ladies of the night."

"Okay. But first tell me how you actually make money from these spiritual spaces. Do people have to pay to pray?"

"The casino pays us, naturally. It's the same as if we rented them an attractive fountain for the lobby or a big tropical fish tank. It embellishes the environment. It elevates the ambience. The design and arrangement of the furnishings, the altars and wall decorations all follow the ancient principles of feng shui. Which is good for luck, you know. Gamblers need luck. It's a pop-up structure, so we own and maintain the space. There's also a donation box for the users of the space, the beneficiaries, to express their appreciation."

"Like a gratuity?"

"You could say that. We have a regional team that comes around every week to empty the donation boxes, and it does add up, yes, indeed. Casinos are full of troubled people looking for spiritual relief and uplift, and when they find it they are grateful and like to express their gratitude. But our main source of income is the monthly rental fee for the space itself. Now, my friend, back to our previous subject."

I'm actually more interested in these pop-up nondenominational chapels than our previous subject, but he's the customer. I ask him again what on the sexual menu interests him. Is he into meat loaf, mac and cheese, peanut butter and jelly sandwiches? Or does he want something more exotic?

A tall, wiry kid in his mid-twenties with a storm cloud in front of his face has settled into a stool three down from my guy and is half listening to our conversation with what looks like disapproval. He has one of those five-day beards designed to demonstrate the high volume of his testosterone flow. I know the kid slightly, name's Enrique. Dominican, I think. Speaks good English with only a slight accent. Comes into the Piano once every ten days or so and stops off for a drink or two before heading into the casino. Doesn't talk much. I believe he's into low-ball roulette. Owns a string of car washes, he told me once, a small-time businessman on the rise, not the type who'd work for someone else. I've never seen him crack a smile. Authority issues, probably. Can't say I'm drawn to him.

I toss him a nod to let him know I'll take his order in a second, but also to cue my guy that if he wants to talk about ladies of the night he should keep it down or else talk in code. For all I know, Enrique's actually an undercover cop. Because of the casino and hotel there's all kinds of plainclothes and undercover cops lurking around, private security guys, local and state, even feds.

Bowtie glances over at Enrique, seems to catch my point and tells me in a low voice that he's interested in some real hot Thai food. "Spicy and burning hot!" he empasizes. Then he turns on his stool 180 degrees, grins at Enrique, winks and says, "Know any place nearby, friend, where a white man can eat Thai or maybe Polynesian?"

Enrique snorts and slips him a slim smile. "You talking Thai men or Thai women? Maybe you're talking fat Polynesian boys," he says and barks a laugh without smiling and shakes his head like he can't believe my guy is a serious person. I'm not sure he's a serious person myself, but his personality sticks to me like Velcro. I'm a bartender, I take people as they come. I don't believe anything they tell me, and I forget them when they go. But something about this guy appeals to me and at the same time turns me totally off. Makes me want to help and hurt him simultaneously. Something about him confuses me.

"White man," Enrique says to himself and snorts again. He turns and shows his back to us. On his neck he's got the tattooed top of a porpoise done in Japanese woodcut style leaping out of his gray silk T-shirt. His shiny black hair is pulled tight into a short ponytail that tickles the porpoise's nose. I go over and take his order, which he gives without looking at me. Vodka martini. Straight up. Ketel One. Extra dry. Three olives.

Enrique knows what he likes.

Bowtie says to him, "What's your name, friend?"

He pulls out his iPhone, makes like he's checking his e-mail. "Enrique," he says. "What do peoples call you, man?" He doesn't look up from his phone. "Whitey?"

"Heck, no! Allyn. Spelled A-L-L-Y-N, pronounced Allen, as in . . . ," he says and looks at the ceiling. "I can't think of any famous Allens. Woody Allen? Anyhow, if spelled with a Y it's a Gaelic name and means 'precious one.' From that you could surmise that I was an only child, Enrique, and you'd be right."

Enrique looks at me and says, "Tell Precious about the Green Door."

"You think?"

"Sure. He want a sexual buffet, he should go to the Green Door. Precious, you can get off any way you want at the Green Door."

This exchange has hooked Allyn at the lip—his head is tilted to one side and his gaze switches from me to Enrique and back to me, like one of us is about to hand him the keys to Sodom and Gomorrah.

Allyn says to me, "That true? Wow! Where is it, the Green Door? What is it, a nightclub? A sex club?"

I explain that it's just a bar located in a minimall on the outskirts of town. It looks like a normal neighborhood sports bar on the outside, but inside at the rear of the place there's this green door, and like the song says, you knock three times and when the door is opened a crack you say, "Joe sent me," and they let you in. "Never been there myself. But I've heard no matter what you're into you can find it behind the green door. Girls in schoolgirl uniforms, cougars, fatties, black, white, and, yeah, Thai. Probably fat Polynesian boys too, and contortionists, rubber suits, whips, ropes, the whole carnival of sex acts. At least that's what I heard. Never been there myself."

I can see he doesn't quite believe me, like it's too good to be true, and I suppose for a guy like him, a Christian dad and husband, a businessman who's never patronized any club nastier than a country club, it is too good to be true. He purses his lips, deep in thought.

"How do you know what they like?" he wonders. "How do you ask them what they want?"

Enrique says, "Fuck, man, they ask you what *you* want! You the fucking customer, man. It's like ordering a drink in a fucking piano bar."

"Got it!" Allyn says. But I can tell he's not at all sure of what he wants. He's probably not even sure of what he wants at home in bed with his wife and waits instead for her to tell him what she wants, then does his manly best to give it to her. Which is why tonight he's wandering down the darkened alleys of his mind to the Green Door. He's spent too many years postponing desire, cultivating fantasies and turning himself into a sexual window-shopper to know what he really wants. Like me, maybe. Only with me it's about life in general and not just sex. Could be that's why the guy both attracts and repels me.

Enrique takes a careful first sip of his martini. He nods with approval and says to me, "Good martini. Tell Precious to keep his wallet in his hand when he's getting off."

I don't want to call him Precious so I just say, "Keep your wallet in your hand when you're getting off, man."

"Got it!" Allyn says again.

"And keep an eye on your watch. That's a nice watch," I say.

"Movado," he says. "Top of the line."

IT'S A FEW MINUTES after six, still early, and Allyn's at work on his fourth Long Island iced tea. It looks like he's not going to make it to the Green Door. Not tonight anyhow. His eyelids are drooping and he's smiling at his reflection in the big mirror behind the bar. Enrique's halfway through his second martini and is unto himself, reading the *Miami Herald* sports page. At the moment, however, despite the hour, the Piano is a happening place. A huge bus has pulled in to the casino and unloaded a couple dozen young giants, most of them black, with twenty or more huge duffels, and a half-dozen normal-sized older men, most of them white. According to their blue and white T-shirts and hoodies, they're the basketball team and coaching staff from Daytona State College. Probably in town for a Suncoast Conference NJC double-A game against Broward College, where there'll be scouts in the stands from Division I teams like Miami or FSU working the junior college circuit. Like the guy said, this is America, and we've got a genius for marketing.

The young giants mingle in the lot by their bus and gawk longingly through the glass doors at the bars and restaurants and casino beyond, while their coaches and handlers check them in and eventually herd them inside the hotel into elevators and send them up to their rooms. As soon as they're gone, the coaches and handlers head straight for the Piano, where they take over a large table in the corner with an unobstructed view of the fifty-two-inch flat-screen opposite the corner where the piano is located. I grab the remote from under the bar and flip the channel off *Judge Judy* onto ESPN, and the whole crew locks onto the screen with mouths open like a nest of baby birds waiting to be fed.

By now the six-to-closing shift has hit the floor, Tiffany and Alicia, the Mutt and Jeff of waitresses, the long and the short of it. Which is a good thing because, in addition to the Daytona State coaching staff, eight or ten slim young dudes have just sailed in. They want champagne. They want to hang out with the piano at the Piano. It's their fourth night here at the hotel and their first night off from performing at the Hard Rock with Cher, who is rumored to have taken the entire top floor of the hotel for herself and is having everything sent up. No one on the staff in any of the casino bars and restaurants can claim to have seen her in person up close except for a few waitresses and some stagehands who glimpsed her when she was being helped on- or offstage by one of her many assistants.

These guys tonight are Cher's backup singers and dancers, and they're lookers, naturally. They're sharp L.A. dressers with perfect rotisserie tans and matching razor-cut haircuts and bodies that won't quit. They're all wearing tight black trousers like toreadors and puffy-sleeved shirts in various pastel colors that should be called blouses, not shirts, and they don't stand around and drink and brag to each other or hit on strangers like most male customers. Instead they wave their hands in the air and talk in staged voices like they're about to break into a Liza Minnelli song. They flounce and bounce like the tiled floor is a trampoline. They're performers and can't stop.

I enjoy listening to them and watching them move. They make me want to sing and dance myself, even if I can't carry a tune and am heavy-footed and have a lousy sense of rhythm. I'm sixty-four and though in my youth had the requisite looks, I never acted the way they do, and now I sometimes wish I had. Not necessarily the gay part, but the loud, dancing, showing-off part. The flash and flamboyance. It looks like fun.

Too late now, though. The flashiest thing I ever did in my youth was audition for a porn movie production company in South Beach when I was thirty-five, divorced and broke. I have a seven-inch dick, but they said it had to be seven and a half, so I took a forty-hour mixology course at the New York Bartending School of South Florida instead. The rest is history. I'm still divorced, but no longer broke. I still have a seven-inch dick, but I'm not thirty-five anymore.

AROUND SEVEN, Allyn seems to break the mirror's hold on his attention. He shakes his head and blubbers his lips like he's waking from a nap and asks for driving directions to the Green

Door. I make him wait while I finish topping off seven flutes of Moët & Chandon for Cher's chorus line. Mutt and Jeff tray the flutes and haul ass. When I give Allyn the directions I say he should be careful driving. After four Long Island iced teas, if the cops stop him no way he'll pass a Breathalyzer.

He sticks out his chest and says, "Are you intimating I'm drunk?"

Enrique folds his paper and says, "Back the fuck off, white bread, or I'll cut your fucking nuts off."

Both Allyn and I say, "Huh?"

It's not clear whose nuts he's threatening to cut off or why. I assume they're Allyn's, but Allyn's giving me a concerned look like he thinks they're mine.

Enrique furrows his brow like he's going to cry. He looks first at me, then at Allyn, and says, "Jesus Christ, I don't know what made me say that. I'm really, really sorry, man. I got this disease, it's like a kind of autism and makes me say shit I don't want to say. I apologize, man."

I tell him no problem, and Allyn says the same, and then, as if to reassure him, Allyn invites Enrique to come along with him to the Green Door.

Enrique politely declines.

Allyn turns to me and says, "How about you, bartender? Care to join me at the Green Door and get sweaty wet with whatever or whomever you fancy?"

It strikes me that Allyn's the one with the disease that

makes people say weird shit they don't mean, except that he means it. "No, thanks, man. I got too much to do here tonight."

Enrique says, "Yeah? What're you doing, killing people?"

"Naw, not tonight," I say. "Actually, my replacement called in sick, so I'm stuck here till closing. Otherwise, yeah, I'd be out killing people." Two can play at this game.

Allyn says, "Or hanging with me at the Green Door!" He lays a hundred on the bar and says keep the change and wobbles from the bar. I deduct sixty for the register and pocket the rest.

Enrique says, "No fucking way that dude's going to end up at the Green Door."

I ask him about this disease he's got, if it comes and goes, or does he have to fight it all the time in order not to say shit he doesn't mean.

"Only time I can forget it is when I'm sleeping. Sometimes I get tired of fighting it, like tonight, and just say fuck it, you know?"

I say I know. But what I really want to know, and don't ask, is how it feels to suddenly blurt out whatever pops into your head. It must be like going behind the green door. It must feel really good to let yourself do that. It must in a way be fun, like being a glittery member of Cher's chorus line swirling across the stage singing "Bang Bang (My Baby Shot Me Down)," which is what they're singing now at the far end of the bar, one of them on the piano, the six others, arms over shoulders, in an actual chorus line, kicking left, kicking right, having a wonderful time performing that goofball of a song for each other and for anyone else in the bar who cares to watch and listen. The coaches all dig it, and Mutt and Jeff grin and watch, and even Enrique seems to like it. And me—maybe especially me, I like it.

IT'S TWO IN THE MORNING before I finally clear everybody out and get the bar washed and locked down and head for the employees' parking lot on the other side of Seminole Way. I'm dragging my bony ass, but if I worked for one of the casino bars instead of the Piano I'd be serving drunks till dawn, so I'm not complaining, just saying.

As I cross the lot toward my Corolla, motion detectors automatically turn on the new ecologically correct LED streetlights, and after I've passed beneath they switch off behind me, one bright light handing me on to the next and then blinking out, all the way across the enormous, nearly empty lot. Palm trees along the sidewalk click and snap in the breeze. A quickie rain shower has cooled the air and clouds of steam rise from the lot as if the pavement is heated from below by fires in the devil's workshop. I've crossed this lot thousands of times and never given it a nod, but tonight for some reason it's spooky. Makes me edgy.

In my head I'm listening to Enrique and Allyn, especially

Allyn, when I arrive at my car and get in. Over the course of the night I had maybe a dozen conversations with customers, some of them interesting, even a couple of them useful. Despite that, I can't remember a one of them, except for my exchange with Enrique and Allyn at the start of the evening, which has stayed with me in a slightly irritating way, like a day-old bee sting.

I'm driving across the lot in the direction of the exit at Lucky Street, still running those guys' words past my inner ears, when my headlights catch three men and a solitary Ford Fusion sedan with its front doors wide open parked at an angle across two adjacent spaces. Caught in the cone of my headlights the three figures are otherwise surrounded by darkness. They act like I'm not there or they don't give a shit that I am. One of the three is jumping around and making big purposeful punching gestures like he's reenacting a WWE wrestling match. He appears to be shouting at the other two, who stand off a few feet and watch him warily as if they're not sure why he's performing for them. They're younger and smaller than he is—red-faced, unshaven Raggedy Andys, a fat one with a long braid who looks like a Seminole and a scrawny one who looks Hispanic. Homeless sunburnt junkies or rosy-faced drunks, I figure. South Florida's largest minority. Next to the sedan they've parked a matching pair of grocery carts stacked with garbage bags filled with all their worldly goods.

The one making the wild gestures I suddenly realize is Allyn, my Long Island iced tea guy, who looks like he's been mugged—bow tie undone, shirt unbuttoned to below his navel, the right sleeve of his jacket half torn off, the suit itself spattered with mud and what looks like spilled red wine or possibly blood, hard to tell in the glare of my headlights. His comb-over is fluffed up like he put his finger in a light socket. He's got a couple of ugly blue bruises on his forehead and a purplish egg swelling below his left eye.

I've stopped my car maybe twenty feet away from him, still inside the parking lot with a high-curbed concrete island between my car and his rental. I reach over to lower the passenger's-side window so I can talk to Allyn. He doesn't look quite sane. But not exactly insane, either.

I get the window all the way down and holler, "Hey, man, you okay? You need help?"

He glances in my direction but doesn't seem to recognize me. "I've had enough help for one night, thank you very much! Unless you're the police and can arrest these two!"

"Allyn, it's me, the guy who sent you to the Green Door, remember?"

The Indian and the Spanish guy edge slowly toward their carts, still keeping a wary eye on Allyn. He looks like he recognizes me now and takes a step in my direction, then sees the two homeless guys about to escape. "Not so fast!" he shouts at them. "We have some unfinished business to settle!"

The two freeze and switch their gaze from him to me and back again. Up to now they've probably been goofing on Allyn, the only guy around who seems crazier than they are. They're thinking they can handle Allyn—they obviously already have— but not the two of us. And maybe I'm carrying a weapon. This is South Florida, after all, and anybody out this late is likely to be armed and could legally shoot them both and say he felt threatened by them. In fact, I have a loaded Smith & Wesson Bodyguard .38 in the glove compartment and could easily take control of this situation if I wanted to. But I don't want to. And I don't feel threatened.

"What's happening here, Allyn?"

"They put something in my drink."

"Who?"

"I don't know. At the Green Door! I woke up in my car, and these two were going through my pockets and taking off my watch."

"What happened at the Green Door?"

"I said, they put something in my drink! Slipped me a mickey! Knockout drops or something!"

"So did you get what you wanted there?"

"I don't remember anything! All I remember is going through the green door. Then suddenly I'm back here in my car and these two are taking my wallet and my Movado. And now I'm going to beat the shit out of them and take my fucking wallet and watch back!"

The Indian and the Spanish guy look mildly pissed is all, like this crazy dude interrupted a friendly parking lot

Thunderbird nightcap. I say, "You guys take his wallet and his watch?"

They shake their heads no. Their eyes are half closed.

I say to Allyn, "Knockout drops? Slipped you a mickey? Give me a break, man. What kinda movies you been watching? You were shitfaced when you left the Piano. You probably never even got out of the parking lot. It's called a blackout, asshole."

I turn to the homeless guys, "Fuck him. He's all yours."

Then, for reasons I can't know or name, I back my car off a short ways. I close the window, and everything comes to a halt, like I'm suddenly unplugged. No power. I just sit there behind the wheel and watch everything unfold like it's happening in high def on a flat-screen with the sound off.

I can't hear him, but I know from Allyn's face and his bulging eyes that he's gone back to yelling at the two homeless guys, and while he yells he dances a weird kind of jig, hopping from one foot to the other with his knees slightly bent. He's flailing his arms and bobbing his head, almost like he's having an epileptic seizure, except his movements are more or less coordinated and intentional. He's gesturing with his hands for them to bring it on, c'mon, man, bring it on!

The Hispanic guy reaches into his front pocket and pulls out a small jackknife and opens the blade.

The Indian guy touches his friend on the arm and says something to him.

As if he hasn't seen the Hispanic guy's jackknife and doesn't see the more serious hunting knife that the Indian has removed from a leather case strapped to his lower leg, Allyn keeps yelling and dancing a fat guy's version of the Ali Shuffle.

The Hispanic guy reaches out with his pocketknife and slashes Allyn's neck from below his right ear to his collarbone, and blood spurts from an artery. Allyn stumbles in his dance and takes one more hop, when the Indian punches his blade into Allyn's belly and jerks it back. With his free hand the Indian pushes Allyn backward two steps. He falls onto the pavement. Blood pours from his mouth. He gurgles, goes silent, kicks both feet once and is still.

The two men wipe their blades on Allyn's pant leg and put their knives away. Not once do they look my way. It's like I'm not there, and in a way I'm not. They grab their grocery carts and disappear into the darkness. I drop my Corolla into gear and cross the parking lot to the exit, turn left onto Lucky Street and drive home.

I go to bed. I fall asleep quickly and sleep without dreams until nearly noon the next day.

A WEEK, maybe ten days later, I'm setting up the bar for the night, shining glasses with a towel, and Enrique strolls in and perches on his usual stool at the bar. Though he's never done anything to make me personally dislike him, I can't say I'm real happy to see him. He reminds me of shit I'd rather not think about.

I nod hello, and he says, "Vodka martini. Straight up. Ketel One. Extra dry. Three olives." While I make his drink he eyes me, like he's auditioning me for a job at a private club, and when I set it in front of him he says, "I appreciate how you make a martini, man."

"Thanks," I say.

When I start to move away, he says, "Kill anybody lately?"

"The fuck you going with that? Why'd you ask me that?"

"Hey, man, I'm sorry! I am really very sorry! Remember I told you sometimes I can't help what I say out loud? It's like I don't even know I'm saying it and peoples can hear it, and then they get all weirded out and upset. I'm really sorry, man."

"Forget it," I say. "I guess we all say and do shit we don't mean."

I step away and go to work making his martini. I bring it to him and shake it down and pour.

"There's some peoples who don't say and do shit that they mean," he says.

"Yeah? Like who?"

"Like that fucking cracker who was here last time, the dude in the bow tie who wanted to go to the Green Door. Remember him, man?"

"What did he not say?"

"That he was a fucking white racist, man. He didn't say that, right? He didn't have to."

"What did he not do?"

"You know the answer to that, man."

"I guess so. But tell me."

"He wanted to fuck a fat Polynesian boy."

"He coulda got what he wanted at the Green Door."

"Nah. He passed out in his car in the parking lot. That dude, man, he never made it to the Green Door," he says, laughing. He lifts his glass and takes the first sip. As the ice-cold vodka hits his brain, he cuts me a smile like he knows everything there is to know about me and says, "And you, you never killed nobody, man."